PAUPER and PRINCE IN HARLEM

A Ross Agency Mystery

DELIA C. PITTS

Praise for the Ross Agency Mystery series

Lost and Found in Harlem

"Rook is a modern, hard-boiled antihero; as the story carries on, he demonstrates ability, humility, decency, and respect and concern for Harlem and its inhabitants… Pitts lovingly illustrates what life is like in a vibrant Harlem, showing people from different walks of life, nationalities, and socio-economic statuses. The neighborhood features prominently not only as a setting, but as a character all its own."

–Kirkus Reviews

Practice the Jealous Arts

"Pitts brings a new and refreshing voice to the murder mystery genre."

–OnlineBookReviews

Black and Blue in Harlem

"Pitts seems to care intensely about her characters, making their troubles and triumphs feel surprisingly poignant. It is this humanity at the core of her novel that provides a spark of hope in a cold-hearted neighborhood of the poor, desperate, and disfranchised. All too often, noir crime stories either curdle into sheer misanthropy or devolve into cheap Raymond Chandler pastiches. Warmth and compassion help elevate this novel far above such stories. In her poignant and hopeful noir mystery, BLACK AND BLUE IN HARLEM, Delia C. Pitts depicts her characters and their lives with insight and compassion."

–IndieReader

For my amazing sons, Adam and Nick, the princes of my heart.

Other Books by Delia C. Pitts

Lost and Found in Harlem

Practice the Jealous Arts

Black and Blue in Harlem

ISBN: 978-1-54399-394-3 (print)

ISBN: 978-1-54399-395-0 (ebook)

AUTHOR'S NOTE: This book is a work of fiction. It depicts individuals from
diverse racial, ethnic, age, gender, and national identities. In particular, complex
transgender characters are presented in this book. None of the characters are
meant to resemble any real persons alive or dead.

CONTENTS

CHAPTER
ONE

"Move, Rook!"

Ambiguous orders never compelled me, even when issued from my boss's beautiful lips. Did Sabrina Ross want me to scoot over on the park bench to give her room to sit next to me? Or did she want me to pick up the damn checker piece, make the double jump, and give this kid the lesson of his short life?

I decided she wanted me to bounce this kid. So, I zapped him good, taking his two forwardmost pieces in a deadly swoop that pushed him back on his haunches. I didn't try to wipe the smile from my face, even as I passed a hand over my brow to smear the sweat dripping there.

"Hey, no fair! She told you that move. No fair, Rook!"

I conceded nothing to this punk's indignation. "You think I didn't have it all figured out? Strategy, my man, strategy."

Brina sat down beside me, leaning her bare brown shoulder against my arm. We knew the dangers of sitting in a city playground at dusk in summer. But we did it anyway. We wanted to escape the clammy corners of our office and the cloying dampness of the neighborhood's cafés. Neither of our apartments had overhead fans to take the sweat off our necks, and the movie theater was an expensive relief we reserved for weekends.

So, we took our drinks and fled to the little park two blocks from her building. There, under dust-draped trees, we joined our neighbors lounging in the favored uniform of city summers: t-shirt and jeans. Old men wore white undershirts with drooping armholes that exposed their wrinkled flanks; middle-schoolers flaunted logos or superheroes; alluring girls tucked jewel-colored tank tops into skimpy shorts. Brina's cut-off jeans reached almost to her knees, but she still gave the teen queens a run for their money in her flimsy tangerine blouse. I stuck with my usual denims, popping the buttons on my work shirt an extra few notches to catch the evening breezes. I was a grown man–I wore my black jeans long. No socks and black sneakers were as cool–and as chill–as I could get this night.

We'd managed to capture an empty bench at a corner of the bustling park. In front of our seat was a concrete pedestal with black squares etched on it, a permanent gameboard installed by the city to offer solace or innocent recreation for Harlem's sweaty hordes. My sometimes checkers partner Zaire Martin had spotted me as I settled and scampered over for a quick match. He was thirteen going on thirty, still wearing baggy nylon shorts and a t-shirt whose ripped hem was either fashionable or desperate. I didn't ask which. Despite his childish outfits, Zaire's high cheekbones framed the tight expression and wary glances of a seasoned veteran of these streets. During our summer of weekly checker sessions, we kept the talk focused on the game. No parents, no school, no business, just checkers. But the boy's eagerness to engage with me revealed a lot about the empty center of his life. Maybe something was missing from mine too.

"Why you take orders from a *woman*, anyway?" Zaire was still ticked off about losing the match, so he let his mini-machismo fly.

I kept my tone even as I set the pieces for another round. "This isn't a woman. This is my boss, Sabrina. You know, Z. I told you about her."

The boy tipped his head to the right, taking a long look at Brina. The slow scan moved from her bushy hair to her naked toes. If he'd been older, I would have taken offense at the frank appreciation in that stare, but Zaire made the gesture comical instead of challenging. "Yeah, Rook, you told me about her. But you didn't *tell* me about her. She's fiiine."

"Acting all surprised like that isn't cool, Z. You're supposed to cover me."

"Fellas, I'm sitting right here. You *do* realize I can hear you, don't you?" Brina's laughing eyes contradicted the pout on her lips, so I knew Zaire and I were okay. She took a long swig from a perspiring bottle of spring water. Before we hit the park, I'd doctored a plastic bottle of ice water with a few drops of bourbon. I should have upped the dose.

"You said your boss was a lady. But you didn't say she was a lady like *this*. I was picturing some chick a whole lot older and a *whole* lot less fly." The kid was undaunted by Brina's presence and determined to get to the bottom of this thicket of adult relationships. The shine over his nut-brown skin matched the gleam in his eyes.

I shrugged and pressed a finger to my lips. "I can't reveal all my secrets up front, Z. You know how it works."

I'd met Brina and her father Norment Ross at the detective agency a little over two years ago. Before that, my pock-marked career had included a stint in the army, plenty of dead-end jobs, and a sorry divorce that ended an even sadder marriage. A down-on-his-luck scrub, I was supposed to meet a *femme fatale* and wind up in the shallow end of a deep pool. Instead, I met Sabrina Ross, a *femme vitale* if ever there was one. Norment invited me to join his little security firm, where I provided the muscle and enough ignorance to lubricate our investigations. Norment brought the soul and the neighborhood contacts. Brina contributed brains, beauty, and a bushel of common sense. I was just damn lucky common sense didn't stop her from inviting me to join her personal life.

Brina cut into our man talk before it went off the rails, pinning the kid with an expert glower. "Is this the Zaire you recommended for that job at the computer repair shop? You said he was smart. But I don't know, I'm not feeling it."

She winked to let Zaire see she was joshing him, her smile expanding to show off brilliant teeth that forced a sharp intake of breath from the boy. He was sprung. In world record time.

"He's just pulling your leg, right, Z?" I stared at the boy, hiding a wink behind another pull from the bottle. Guiding this kid strained my childcare skills. If I'd owned any parenting muscles, they'd have frayed weeks ago.

"Yeah, I'm just messing. Like Rook say."

Brina lowered her voice to a formal whisper and squared her shoulders to look straight at Zaire. "Mr. Arnold needs somebody reliable to help him stock equipment and clean up the store every night. You think you could be the right man for the job?"

Zaire knew he'd fallen into an interview here on the park bench, and he rose to the occasion. "Yeah, I'm interested in that computer job. I can handle it. I like messing with computers, electronics, stuff like that. I'd do good work in Mr. Arnold's shop."

Before he could expand on his resumé, a whistle darted across the park, causing Zaire to jerk his head in its direction. A thin teenager waved, then beckoned with a rapid gesture suggesting urgency.

Zaire reached for his backpack and stood from the table. "That's my boy, Whip. Gotta go. I'll check you later, Rook. Nice to meet you, Miss Sabrina." Zaire trotted through the gathering gloom toward his friend. A slap on the shoulder then a high five completed their exchange of greetings.

"He's a nice kid, Rook. I can see why you like him. Tough, smart, funny. Reminds me of you." She looked at the teens in conversation across the dusty grass enclosure. Lowering her chin, she murmured, "I want to tell you something."

"Sure. Shoot"

"Not here. Later." Brina wriggled as if a sudden chill had tickled her shoulders. Then a smile dashed across her mouth. "Let's make that computer job happen for Zaire."

"From your lips to Old Man Arnold's ears." I demonstrated my agreement by planting a peck on Brina's cheek. She swiveled her head to answer with a better kiss. But we never got that far.

Four gunshots zipped across the innocent playground, pinging like chimes against the metal legs of the swing set.

Shouts and children's cries ripped through the sultry twilight enclosing the park. Two more bullets screamed by our ears. Bodies thumped to the grass as the acrid stink of rubber scraping asphalt floated along the ground. I jerked Brina from our bench and threw myself on top as her cheek hit the sidewalk. My weight on her, I raised my torso to look around. After the first shriek, a naked burst of energy thrust the crowd of teens and adults in all directions.

Through the tangle of running legs, I spotted Zaire's baggy shorts. He was standing stock still, his hand on the strap of the green satchel slung over his shoulder. The rifle's next report was muffled and distant, but its result was devastating: a red flower bloomed from the boy's smooth brown forehead. Zaire's round face registered first shock, then scorn as he crumpled. Knees crunched on gravel. Then his chest and forehead hit the cement, murder's payload delivered before he landed.

Summer dusk brings different kinds of death, depending on where you are. In the fields of south Texas where I grew up, fireflies come out as the sun sets. You can capture them in your glass jars to light the walk home before they sputter and die. In fancy suburbs, twilight encourages deer to career across the streets, where cars strike them down. And in cities, hidden snipers take advantage of the dwindling haze to cut off their prey with a burst of bullets, delivering death from steel vaults on wheels.

This night's gunfire blew an ugly trench through the thick humidity. From my position on top of Brina, I rotated my head, looking for the source of the bullets. I saw a white van, maybe silver. Maybe the sniper's vehicle. I thought I saw the barrel of an automatic jut from a rear window. Or maybe it was a dark arm brandishing a pistol. Not sure. But I did catch the destruction of Zaire Martin. Even from one hundred yards away, I knew he was dead before his bare knees hit the ground.

To his left was another boy, the friend Zaire had called Whip. Same age as Zaire but taller, same green backpack on his shoulder. This second kid didn't display the terror that spurred the ruckus swirling around him. Instead, a strange determination froze into a scowl on his face. Whip turned with deliberate calm, shouldered the second strap of his heavy backpack, and stalked through the crowd toward the edge of the park.

I jumped to my feet and dragged Brina onto the bench, two hands pressing on her shoulders. Grabbing her chin to underline my instructions, I told her to call 911, then return to her apartment.

Brina pushed my hand from her face. "But, what about you? Where're you going?" Anger shoved aside the fright in her eyes.

My next words would add confusion to the mix. "I'm following that kid over there." I pointed to the retreating figure of the boy with the green backpack. "He's got something to hide. Or something to say about this shooting. Either way, I want to find out what he knows."

"It's not safe. You could get hurt."

"Brina, you heard the van. You know the drill. Snipers have cut out. Cops arrive soon. No more shooting at this corner for the night. This is the safest square block in Harlem right now."

She looked skeptical, but calculation crept across her face. She knew I was right. About the safety of our immediate setting at least. I didn't tell her I'd seen Zaire cut down in the twilight.

"Go to your apartment."

"Where will you be?"

"I'll catch up with you there." Breath burst from me in short spurts, panic and urgency propelling my thoughts. This wasn't my case, not yet. But I wanted it to be. Zaire was murdered and this boy Whip had answers. If I continued arguing with Brina, the kid would melt into the shadows.

Tears dripping through specks of gravel on her cheeks, Brina sputtered and reached for my hand. But I jerked away and dashed through the gloom as dusk condensed over the little park. This retreating figure was my only clue. I refused to lose another kid to the night.

CHAPTER
TWO

I reined the trot to a fast walk after two blocks of tailing the kid with the green backpack.

My bum left foot demanded the slower pace; Usain Bolt was my spirit animal, but a roadside bomb in Iraq had destroyed two toes. And killed my pal Charlie Bunche. Nothing I could do about Charlie or the foot; neither forgetting nor running was an option now. So, leftover guilt and a speedy limp propelled me around the neighborhood.

The kid stayed one hundred yards ahead. Even at a distance, I could see muscles rippling over the length of his jaw. He didn't look frightened or worried. Fury overrode other emotions, setting his face into a bleak mask. Anger drove me too. Zaire deserved a better life than the one he'd been dealt: he should have checked out seventy years from now, dozing under a red beach umbrella, watching pretty granddaughters build sandcastles. Vengeance was ugly, but if I could win a portion for Z, it would be enough.

Head down, the kid kept charging. We passed empty storefronts, shuttered groceries, a Duane Reade, two nail salons, and grimy restaurants hawking fried chicken, deli sandwiches, burritos, and shawarmas. At this steady pace he wasn't wandering, but aimed at a definite destination. Home or hideout, that stop was partial answer to the quiz zooming through my head. He must have spotted me blocks back; there weren't many tall, skinny, mixed-race guys limping on the boulevard at that hour. He could have outrun me any time he wanted. This chase suited his purpose for some reason. But dodging wasn't his game. If he was determined to be followed, I was just as fixed on catching him.

On the move, I called Brina to check she'd made it home. Her voice trembled as the greeting spilled; at least I wasn't sprawled on a curb with a bullet in my temple. But after another soft phrase, she came at me pissed and spoiling for a fight. I promised we'd square for a good battle as soon as I got to her place. She calmed again, even huffed a short laugh. I disconnected before she could rev up for round two.

When the kid passed a second pawn shop, my bum foot screamed for an end to this trek. Answering that prayer, he veered off the sidewalk and dashed into an abandoned warehouse. I waited a beat to give him a head start.

The redbrick Pallas warehouse was a familiar landmark. I passed it at least twice a week on my rounds through the neighborhood. Driftwood gray boards blocked the first-floor windows, but the upper story's openings were vacant and bare. Bright graffiti tags ballooned at shoulder height along the façade: "Ramón" and "Dragger" were sure proud of their flamboyant scrawls. Norment Ross told me the building had a history as colorful as its current décor. It had been a brewery, then a paint factory in the 1930s, then the short-lived Yum-mee Bakery. A fur storage business hung on into the '60s. In the '70s, a small outpost of the garment industry had planted itself in Harlem: Pallas Sportswear, Inc. made pants, suits, and dresses under contract for downtown apparel houses.

The business lasted a decade. Before George Pallas went bankrupt, he carved his family name in limestone blocks over the door of the warehouse. The name was fifteen feet above street level, too high for the graffiti artists to maul when cokeheads and horse fiends took over the building searching for a quiet shooting gallery. The Pallas company symbol, a seven-foot-tall Greek goddess in a white toga, still guarded the building entrance. The paint of her white forehead had crackled, jade slashes outlined her mouth, and a purple pedicure tipped her naked toes. An owl, dappled green and lilac, perched on her shoulder. Hundreds of addicts passing through this door had rubbed the goddess's breast for luck until her gown's painted folds blurred to mouse gray. Just after the turn of the century, when the homeless crowd moved in, some genius junkie had dubbed the Pallas warehouse, "The Palace."

The track-star kid with the green backpack disappeared into this shadowy entrance, so I followed. I tapped the Pallas goddess for good luck, then jerked a doorknob to the left of the tiny vestibule. It was locked. Then I kicked a door on the right. Dirt shimmied, paint flaked, but no joy.

The tall staircase straight ahead was my last choice. The flight of steps was rickety and uneven; I pressed my palm to the brick wall as I advanced. Past the door frame at the second-floor landing, I paused to catch my breath. A broad floor of bleached wooden planks stretched a city block before me. Wind gusted through the high arches lining both sides of the broad space. No panes barred the immense windows and the unfiltered moonlight cast bold silver buttresses that seemed to prop the double height walls. Dust, humidity, and the stillness of the space reminded me of the majestic cathedral I sometimes visited on Fifth Avenue. This place was St. John the Divine minus the droning undercurrent of worship and hope.

Figures clustered at regular intervals along both walls. The distances separating the huddled groups enforced a makeshift privacy. Mattresses, barrels, metal folding chairs, and wooden crates served as furniture. People gathered around empty oil drums to laugh and talk. Though energy crackled between them, no one touched. No backslapping, no gentle shoves, or joking taps on the chin or shoulder. No one was joshing here. Connections between these men seemed formal and correct, the restraint of a genteel fraternity, rather than the rowdiness of a neighborhood bar or social club. These tall barrels were hearths at rest; dark and empty now, they would provide fire for light and warmth in the winter.

Fifty people stirred in the warehouse, mostly black men with dashes of other races salting the crowd. I kept my eyes low to study a group gathered halfway down the room's great length, looking for my quarry.

I saw him before he spotted me. The boy was crouched in front of a mattress, balancing on the balls of his feet in apparent ease, nodding at a man's animated conversation. The man was seated on the bare pad, his short legs thrust straight in front of him. The boy's keen eyes tracked the movements of the man's face, and both their mouths gaped in amusement. Despite the sudden horror he'd witnessed in the park, the kid was happy here. At home.

I paced toward the pair, shoulders up, stride long, movements overt. I wanted information from them, and that required trust. Or at least a lack of fear. Even though night temperatures blasted past eighty, the old man was wrapped in a purple wool overcoat and wore thick gloves. He jammed a gold knit cap over bushy gray hair as if fighting his own personal winter. The moon slanting through the high windows captured him in a bolt of silver light that made his face and figure glow like a sculpture in a museum. His skin was dark and smooth as a river-polished stone. Newspapers and magazines were stacked to one side of the mattress. At the other edge was a grocery cart filled with flattened cardboard boxes, folded clothing, kitchen and garden tools, and a busted boombox.

Though he was facing the boy, the man's milky brown eyes focused on the far end of the hall. I walked in a wide circle around the pair, passing through several clusters of people. I lost sight of the two as I rounded a cast-iron column. By the time I got to within twelve feet, the kid had vanished into the crowd.

I crouched at eyelevel before the old man, who scooted over on the mattress to give me room. As I settled, I imitated his posture, thrusting my legs straight in front. Side by side, it was easy to take his measure: his legs extended no further than my knees. He was perhaps five feet tall to my six one.

A foggy tenor voice slid from the moth-eaten coat. "Whip tells me you the dude been tailing him. Are you?"

He tilted his large head. It might have been a trick of the light, but gears seemed to shift behind his eyes, snapping a piercing assessment of me. The moon turned his pupils molten, like drops of mercury slipping from a broken thermometer.

"Is Whip the boy's name?" That's what Zaire had called him, but I didn't reveal it. The man nodded, waiting for my explanation. "He witnessed bad things in the park this evening. You know anything about that?" Not offering much, but since I knew so little, taking that stance was easy.

"No more than what he told me. A drive-by shooting took out a young kid. Whip ran, you trailed him six blocks. That's what I heard tell. You got anything else?"

"No." In the clash of my ignorance and his stubbornness, we'd come to an impasse. A direct approach might work. The straight ask could win an honest answer. "I'd like to talk with Whip. You know where he disappeared to?"

"You a cop?" Without a hitch, he slipped into defender mode, countering my question with his own. Lawyer role, or maybe father. Hard to judge which this soon.

"No. Whip can tell you about my foot." In the few minutes it had taken me to circle the grand warehouse the old tramp must have noticed my limp. "You think the cops are into charity hires these days?"

His high hooting laugh startled two men leaning against the windowsill to the right of our mattress. They stood and frowned as if the loud noise broke some Hooverville code of etiquette. But when they saw who made the racket, they ducked their heads and tipped fingers to their brows in salute. Judging by their gesture, I was talking with a weighty elder in the community.

"You got that right, mister. Hire the handicapped ain't po-po's thing." I smiled too, joining in the joke, even at my expense. He squinted to study me. "So, if you ain't a cop, what's your stake in this business? You just a noble citizen with a curiosity itch?"

"The way he ran, Whip looked like he was in trouble."

"So?" His theatrical shrug sent a lilac plume of dust into the air between us.

"I'm a private detective. I thought I could help. That's all."

"You a private dick? Hunh. I never met one of you people up close." When he leaned in, a chewy mix of hot dogs, sauerkraut, and whiskey drifted on his breath. "You make any kinda living like that?"

"Not much." I unrolled the sleeves of my denim shirt so he could inspect their frayed cuffs. Then I laid my left ankle over the other knee to show the shredded rubber outsole of my black sneaker. My threadbare style was grounded in scarcity, not fashion.

He grunted in acceptance and gracefully changed the subject from my poverty. He pointed at my sneakers and huffed a short laugh. "That's what they used to call you people– 'gumshoes.' I guess it still fits. You got a name?"

"Call me Rook. And you?"

"I'm Eddie." He pulled off a stiff leather glove to shake hands. Like his head, his hand was outsize for his slim torso and legs. His scarecrow body seemed made from parts collected over years of careful scavenging.

I squeezed as hard as he did. "Nice to know you, Eddie." Palms soft, no farm or factory callouses. But the fingernails had the horny texture and mottled brown color of an old turtle shell. "You a relative of Whip? He seemed to head right to you when he got in trouble."

"We're all related here, family one way or another." The old man waved his arm in an arc to indicate the long expanse of the camp and the rag-bag collection of people it sheltered.

"Whip been coming here, on and off, for near on five months now. I took him under my wing when he first arrived, and we been fast friends ever since."

I dragged my gaze over the crowd, then looked him in the eye. "If you think he could use it, tell Whip I'm ready to help."

"We all need a little help now and then. The hard part is getting youngbloods like Whip to recognize when that needful moment comes along." Eddie shook his head at the reckless ways of youth. "You raise any kids, you know all about that kind of foolishness, don't you? But I guess we was all stubborn mules once, wasn't we?"

I pulled a Ross Agency business card from my jeans pocket and pressed it flat on my thigh before handing it over. "Could you give him this? He can get in touch with me when and how he chooses."

Eddie studied the card's shiny black surface and traced a finger around the bold red outline of the unblinking eye in the middle. He scratched a nicotine-stained nail over my name, checking the height of the embossing. Then he slipped the card under the knit cap and into the thicket of his hair for safe keeping.

"Sure, I'll see he gets it, Rook. What he does with it is up to him. But Whip's a smart 'un. He'll figure it out."

Our conversation had reached its natural end; we'd each given as much as we were prepared to share on first meeting. The weariness draping over me was equal parts physical exhaustion and delayed reaction to Zaire's gruesome death. The old man hadn't witnessed it, but still he absorbed my spent state. So, we said nothing further, sighing together as the shafts of light piercing the great hall turned from tin to silver to royal purple.

I was about to hoist my weight from the mattress when a new figure entered the scene.

A striking woman flounced in front of us like she owned the Palace. Or at least the mattress. She was as tall as me, with matted hair tangled into black dreadlocks trailing almost to her waist. Her mahogany skin stretched across sharply angled cheekbones and a high forehead. Under layers of gauzy pastel fabric, her skin glistened in the moonlight like an oiled wooden idol.

"Well, look what the cat dragged in!" A loopy grin split her face. She was talking about me, although her eyes were pinned on Eddie. The newcomer's buoyant mood couldn't be dampened by the morose atmosphere billowing around her home. "Or, get a load of the good-looking cat what got dragged in!"

Her eyes slanted toward me and the saucy song spouted from her like a geyser. "Hey, good-looking! Whatcha got cooking?" By the end of this snippet, her warm gaze was full on me, not so much questioning my unexplained presence as glad for the audience.

The old man snapped to cut off the song. "Odette, this is Rook. He's come about Whip."

"I remember Rook and those crazy gorgeous eyes from the last time he was here. How ya doing, Rook?" The bent grin widened as she cackled at me. Two teeth were missing from the lower row but that gap only added to the daffy twinkle of her smile.

13

"Odette, this man ain't never been here in all his born days." Eddie's drawl was patient, as if the conversation, or its near neighbor, was one they had plowed through many times before.

His companion was undeterred by the intrusion of reality. She pointed a graceful finger at my face. "Sure, he has. Look at those fine eyes. I'd know them beauties anywhere. Say, Rook, why didn't you bring your cousin Thurman for another visit? Just like old times."

And the woman launched into a new song, inspired by the phrase or my nonexistent cousin, or some other phantom in her cloudy mind. Dreadlocks swinging, taffeta rustling in time to the plaintive tune, Odette sang and waved her long hands to conduct an invisible orchestra. "Seems like old times, having you to walk with..."

Though her band was invisible, the audience could hear Odette loud and clear. And wasn't happy about the noise. "Hey, pipe down, Princess. Why dontcha?" The shrill gripe rang across the warehouse from a group fifty yards away.

Odette whirled to identify the complainer, but no one raised his head. Perhaps in response, Eddie's tone sharpened as he turned up the volume. "Odette, knock it off. We're not in the mood."

"Well, I can see that, killjoy. I was trying to put you people in the mood." She made air-quotes around the mocking repetition. "But I guess that won't work." With pursed lips, she continued humming her cabaret song until she had completed all the verses and made a deep curtsey despite the silence from Eddie and me.

Undaunted by her companion's stiff words, Odette flung a large canvas duffel bag at his feet. She dropped onto the mattress between me and Eddie, a confusing blend of sweet lavender and onions wafting from her billowing skirts.

"You hungry, Eddie?" With a flourish, she pulled an assortment of food from the bag. Odette's scavenged dinner included club sandwiches in wax paper, falafel wraps, bare hot dogs, and two small bags of corn chips.

Eddie's eyebrows bounced. "I could sure do with a taste."

If this was a peace offering, it worked. Eddie seemed energized by this bounty and the two polished off the entire feast. They asked once in a rushed whisper if I wanted a share, and when I shook my head, they gobbled my portion without ceremony. For dessert, Eddie pulled from under the mattress a half-pint bottle of Four Roses bourbon and passed it to his companion. He didn't offer me any.

When they'd eaten, Odette spoke to me again. "You said you came looking for Whip. You from the child services too?"

"No. There was some trouble in the park a few hours ago. I thought he could use help." Odette might know something of value, so I made my voice soft to encourage after-dinner conversation.

She knew something, but its value was obscure. "There was a lot of you child services people around tonight. I saw those two men with the same exact face, the ones who I seen with Whip a time or two before. In a white van. They was hanging around the park this evening just like you was. You with child services, right?"

Eddie swung his head from side to side. "Odette, Mr. Rook here don't need none of your fantasy tripping tonight. You didn't see no two men with the same exact face. You know that's impossible."

"But I did. I *did* see them two men with one face, Eddie." The woman's lids screwed together as the eyeballs jumped behind them, reviewing a scene only she could identify.

"And you know he's not with child services 'cause he just told you. So, stop saying it when you know it's not true."

"I'm not tripping, Eddie. You know I'm not." Tears twinkled like diamonds on the tips of her dusty lashes.

Eddie relented, reaching out to pat Odette's knee. "I know you not tripping, baby. Not tripping. Just thinking about that east side, west side song, right, Odette?"

That invitation seemed to lift his companion's mood once again. Inspired, off she went, digging deep into her grab bag of Americana classics. Her voice mellowed to a soft lilt, turning the bouncy tune into melancholy lament "…Tripped the light fantastic on the sidewalks of New York."

None of us were in any condition to dance, so I took this as my cue to leave them to their private songbook communing. I pushed off the mattress.

Eddie stood too, his head rising only chest high. When his long coat flopped around him, I saw what had been hidden beside him on the mattress: a lumpy green backpack decorated with black lightning bolts. The same bulging satchel Whip had carried from the park. Identical to the one Zaire had hoisted on his shoulder seconds before a bullet cut him down.

Eddie saw me check the bag. He took a step to the left to hide it. This backpack was out of bounds for our conversation. But the old tramp was wrong: the backpack might not be my business, but it was a clue in my case. For the time being, however, Eddie had given me enough to go on. He'd made the connection to the boy. The next move was Whip's.

My instinct and groaning foot begged to head home; a solitary swoon across my empty bed called. But I resisted the desire and went to Brina's apartment like I'd promised. A new wash of sweat drenched my shirt as I trudged the streets toward her place. Damp and sticky, the fabric rubbed the crooks of my elbows and the ridge of my neck like a soiled napkin. Even the rivets in my jeans heckled and poked. I was covered with the grime of Zaire's playground death and the dismal dust of the vagrants' camp. I needed a shower to wash off the dirt and Brina's trembling attention to soothe me into the night. I got both.

CHAPTER
THREE

The sweet grassy scent of chamomile tea drifted through the bedroom, rousing me from sleep. Brina usually enjoyed a stiff jolt of Ethiopian Highland coffee in the morning, so the mild herbal mix was a mystery worth leaving bed to solve.

When I padded into the kitchen, I found her leaning two elbows on the counter next to the refrigerator, dragging a tea bag in circles around her red mug. She was showered, brushed, dressed in purple shorts and an embroidered linen shirt, ready to face the day. I'd managed to scrounge a pair of boxers. My approach prompted her to shovel six spoonfuls of grounds into the coffee-maker before taking a sip from her weak infusion.

"What's up with the herbal tea?" Morning gumminess clogged my throat. I expected Brina to snap a brisk greeting as correction, but she stared at her cup and shrugged.

"My stomach was rough after yesterday. I wanted something soothing this morning. So, chamomile."

"Yeah, yesterday was tough." I kissed her temple, then slid around her to pour coffee for myself. I brought the steaming mug to the counter and leaned toward Brina, my shoulder pressing against hers.

Her voice wavered near me, so soft I had to duck my head to hear: "You think the cops will catch them?"

"The people who killed Zaire? I doubt it. They have zero clues and witnesses with a playground full of reasons to avoid snitching. Nobody will risk their own lives or the lives of their kids to tell what they saw."

She sat her mug next to the cell phone on the counter. "But you'll keep trying, won't you?"

"I have to. Zaire was my friend. I owe it to him to track down his killer."

"I figured." Brina tore a corner from the yellow tag as she steered the tea bag in another circle. She squared her shoulders and her voice rose with the next words. "I'm late."

I glanced at the cell phone. "It's only 7:15. You missed an appointment already?"

Her barking laugh caught me like a slap on the cheek. "That's what you go with? I say I'm late and you drop a line from a TV sit-com script?"

"Oh, you mean? I didn't see... I mean, how...?" My lips popped and words gargled in my throat. I swallowed a mouthful of coffee to drown the questions.

"Yeah, my period's late."

"How late?"

"Ten days."

"Are you sure? How do you know?" I should have squelched the babbling with more coffee, but the mug stayed glued to the counter.

Brina's lips tilted at the left corner, smiling to forgive my idiocy. "I keep track. That's how I know. Little dots on my calendar. Ever since high school. I'm regular as a clock. Always have been. But this month, things are off."

"Have you... I mean, you know... tested with those kits or something? To be sure?"

"Not yet. I want to wait a few more days." She blew a long gust of air, ruffling the wisps of steam over her mug. Creases bracketing her mouth deepened and she nibbled at flakes of gray skin on her lower lip. "I'll do the test. Soon."

"Is this what you wanted to tell me last night in the park?"

18

"Yeah, this is it." Her eyes scraped across my face, from eyes to mouth to chin.

"I don't know what to say, Brina." I scrabbled my fingers across the counter until I could grab her pinkie. I raised her hand to my heart, then placed four kisses in her palm.

"Then don't say anything yet." I wrapped my arms around her, pressing her head into my chest. Her phrases rumbled through my body. "Not until we know for sure."

We'd run to the end of our words, so swaying together in sunlit dust motes drifting before the kitchen window seemed the best thing to do. Until the cell buzzed and the police called us back to the world.

"Yes, Officer Rubin, I'm Sabrina Ross... Yes, I called 911 last night." Eyes rolling, Brina pointed at the phone in mock horror. I gave the cut-throat sign, but she plunged on.

"I can tell you what I saw. But it's not much... Okay, sure, confirming what you got from other witnesses is good. I was on a bench near the south end of the park. About eight-fifteen we heard wheels screech... No, not stopping, more like fast turning around a corner, that kind of sliding noise the rubber makes when it's burning asphalt. The sound was heavy, maybe from a limo, maybe a van... No, I didn't see the vehicle, only heard it... The gunshots? Like popcorn, only deeper, muffled, oily thuds is the best way I can describe them... My co-worker pushed me onto the ground then. After that, all I saw was feet scrambling in every direction... His name is Shelba Rook... Yes, he's here with me... Sure, hold on. I'll get him."

Co-worker, indeed. Not talking, not before I finished my coffee. I wagged my head. Brina passed the phone to me anyway. Our work day had begun, even if I was still half naked. Georgette Rubin's voice was fresh and bouncy, no doubt fueled by a double dose of frosted flakes and an iced caramel latté-to-go. She sounded eager to try those fancy interview techniques she'd learned at the police academy two weeks ago. I was trapped, an ideal candidate for the experiment.

"That's right, I was there last night, Officer... Yeah, I saw a van climb the curb and approach the playground... Yeah, it was white, or maybe silver... Semi-automatic fire broke from the rear window, driver's side...

I saw one kid go down. Others may have been hit too... The kid was Zaire Martin... Yes, like the African country... I knew him. We played checkers. He was thirteen, maybe fourteen years old...No, I don't know his people. No idea about his parents or family... No, I don't have an address for him."

I didn't tell Officer Rubin about the other kid, Whip, or my hike to the homeless camp. I didn't tell her I was working the case from my own angle. I didn't tell her about the tramps Eddie and Odette or the fistful of hunches I'd developed after talking with them. As a brown boy without a father growing up in San Marcos, Texas, I'd learned the survival essentials: respond to the bare intent of official questions. Nothing more. Don't smile, don't laugh, don't stare, don't embellish. And never volunteer anything.

The heartfelt thanks of Officer Georgette Rubin boosted us to the agency office by nine. Brina took a second NYPD phone call at nine-forty. After a ten-minute chat, she reported my pal Detective Archie Lin threatened to visit our office in the afternoon to square my story of the shooting with what his crew of forensic experts had gathered at the scene.

I liked Archibald Lin. I respected his brains and his experience. Being Chinese-American in the NYPD wasn't the same as being mixed race anywhere in America. But whenever our similarities threatened to spike the friendship, our differences jerked us to equilibrium. He never tolerated my brooding. Sometimes I rode deep into the bi-cultural, bi-lingual, bi-racial complexities of my life. In grade school, I was the border crossing made flesh: too brown for the white kids, too yellow for the black kids; too Mexican for the Anglo kids, too gringo for the Mexican kids. Even grown and far from sunbaked south Texas, I still wallowed in the old days from time to time. There was something comforting about those ancient beefs and schoolyard brawls, when finding your tribe just meant sizing up the other team's football skills. Now, when I peddled into my own private swamp, Archie Lin threw a crowbar into the spokes of my BS bicycle and pulled me out. That mulatto morass didn't suit me, he said. Good friend that he was, Archie always appreciated my kinky jokes and drank less bourbon than me. Private eye and cop, we fit together. Besides height, we shared high yellow skin and black hair. If he'd lose sixty pounds, lift a barbell, and visit a decent barber, we'd even look alike. In his dreams.

In the past two years, we'd worked several knotty cases together: Archie's tenacity matched my instincts in an off-beat collaboration. And since he'd had the smarts to marry Brina's best friend, Pinky Michel, I even admired his taste in women. But now I wanted no part of sparring with him in a game of Twenty Questions about the shooting in the park. Straight questions demanded honest answers. That was my motto. The only escape from the Archie trap was avoidance. I was too footsore and anxious to enjoy him stir-frying my brains.

I considered skipping the office altogether to evade Archie. But now, with a million questions between Brina and me, hooky seemed a particularly careless play. Flake on the job, scrub as a father. Office it was. With no excuse to escape the cops on my trail, the day threatened to dissolve into a puddle of uneasy recitations, moist boredom, and listless typing at overdue expense reports. I was lucky Brina wasn't my only boss.

"You got anything on your docket today, Junior?" Norment Ross's question splashed like a chilled bucket of water across the steamy air of my office.

I flicked beads of sweat from my chin before I answered. "Nothing I can't ditch."

I wanted the impression of cool control to waft from me, so I kept both feet planted on the lower drawer of my desk and leaned back in my chair: I was a man who'd mastered the challenges of this hectic life, the conqueror of his fate, the rugged champion of his future.

But I couldn't hold onto the pose. Breaking the illusion, I sat up and yapped like the last puppy in the pet store window. Tongue flapping, tail wagging, begging to be adopted. "You need me for something, Norment?"

He unfurled a giant handkerchief from his back pocket and dragged it over his shiny face. The sweat left damp splotches on the white cloth. "Got a little case needs keen eyes and a tough backside. You think you got what it takes?"

"Stakeout? I'm your man, Norment." Eagerness squeezed my voice higher than usual.

It wasn't really an invitation, since he was my boss. But following orders allowed me to escape Archie Lin's questions. And an afternoon dawdle in Norment's air-conditioned Ford Taurus beat sweltering at my desk in front of a blazing computer screen.

We'd driven ten blocks when Norment slipped into a shady slot on a quiet residential street.

The sidewalk was broad and empty, the heat had driven pedestrians off the cement. They hid in shade where they could find it: inside laundromats, liquor stores, pizza joints, and greasy wings parlors. Store clerks were lenient, giving the steamed loungers a pass on purchases in exchange for good will and quiet. Nobody grumbled and nobody moved. Without foot traffic on this side street, the row of brownstone staircases was monotonous in its bareness. The only variation in the clean-swept vista was a front stoop which featured a giant pot of red geraniums.

"What's the assignment, Norment?" When he made no move to exit the car, I reached to yank the lever, pushing the seat back to give me room to stretch out full length. I waited for the boss's orders. "You were awful quiet on the drive over here." I wondered if Brina had spilled her news to her father, but decided she'd wait until she had confirmation. No need to poke that hornet's nest until necessary.

It was too hot to lift an arm, so Norment responded by nodding his bald head in the direction of the windshield. "You see that porch, the one with the pot?"

I admitted I'd noticed it. Norment rolled the sleeves of his lilac linen shirt until each folded neatly over an elbow. He loosened the knot in his white tie and fished a new handkerchief from his pocket. He ran the crisp cloth along both sides of his glistening head, then once straight down the center of his face over the damp bristles of his snow-white goatee.

Without looking me in the eye, he answered: "That's what we're watching this afternoon."

"A flower pot? That's the case?" I squinted but kept my eyes on the glove compartment.

"Yep. That's it, Junior. You think you up to this assignment? Or is it too much for your hard-boiled brains to handle?"

"We're on surveillance of a bunch of *flowers*?"

"Not just any flowers. Geraniums. And not just geraniums, but red ones. And not just red geraniums." His grin heated the interior ten more degrees. "Red geraniums that move themselves back and forth on that front stoop at least twice a week. For the past four weeks. That's what we here to watch."

I craned my eyes toward the flowers, then back to Norment. "You're pulling my leg, right?"

"If I pull your leg, I'll tug on the bum one. So, when I *do* yank it, son, you best believe I'll pull so hard your old granny'll feel it way out west in that Texas scrub country you crawled out of."

Norment's chuckle encouraged me to admire his joke, but still I felt a tiny twinge in my bad foot. I pushed a reply through gritted teeth. "Okay. Then fill me in on the case."

Norment settled in his seat, lifting his shirt with rapid jerks to generate a breeze across his torso. He took a deep breath before diving into his story. "Day before last I got a call from Marietta Lowery. I've known Miz Lowery for almost twenty-five years, ever since she and her husband hired me to look into the background of the girl their son intended to marry."

He flicked beads of sweat from the notch at his throat and continued. "Turned out the girl was a straight up, stone cold thief. Chick shoplifted since she was in fifth grade, hit her stride in high school, and kept on with her sticky-finger ways right through college. Everything not nailed down, that girl stole. Lipsticks, perfume, belts, wallets, blouses, earrings. Cops nabbed her a few times. But the store owners always dropped charges on account of Miss Thing was cute as a kitten in ear muffs."

Norment smiled at the eternal marvel of feminine double-dealing. "I gave the Lowerys the ugly details about that girl, but their son ignored my report. Love'll do that to a man. Especially love for a pretty woman. Foul 'im up but good. Last I heard the Lowery boy and his thief-bride were living the high life in Pensacola, with two kids in college and a third starting med school."

Norment paused for a moment of silent appreciation for the whimsy of life. Then he shrugged and summed up the moral of the sermon. "Just shows even faced with the facts, people gonna pick their own path. A good lesson for us all, Junior. Us private eyes can't play God, no matter how much we think we know."

No quarrel from me. I hoped he was right. Not being able to fix all the ills of the world gave me freedom to probe and meddle and work for the best outcome. If Norment was right, then maybe some of that responsibility I always carted around could melt off in this scorching sun.

Heat fused this pardon and my memories of poor Zaire's death into a drowsy vapor. I unfastened another shirt button to let cold air blow over my sweaty undershirt. I sank lower in the seat. After the night's long trek to the Palace, I was weary. The dry ache of exhaustion crawled through my back, shins, ankles, and feet. I rested my head against the sticky seat and closed my eyes for a beat.

As stupor swam over me, Norment intervened. "Before you get too comfy, son, reach into the trunk and pull out the cooler I got back there." He dropped his voice into announcer bass: "Miller Lite is the right beverage for afternoon surveillance. Hits the spot without weighing you down." He paused to let the pitch settle. "Think they'd hire me to do a TV commercial for 'em?"

"Sure, Norment. You sold me." I retrieved the insulated box from the trunk and put it on the back seat. Norment had loaded the cooler with twelve cans of beer, ready for a long day's stakeout into night. I'd never hurry Norment through his presentation of the case; he could draw out a shaggy dog story with the best fable tellers. But still I prodded. "So, Mrs. Lowery called you last week, did she?"

"Yeah, like I said. She called asking for our help with a puzzle. Her husband passed six years ago. But she stayed on in the old place, even though it's big enough to house a battalion. Everything was quiet until this summer, she said. Then in June she started noticing something funny with her red geraniums."

We were getting to the flowers at last. I leaned forward, pulling my shirt from the gummy leather cushion.

Norment raised his eyebrows when he saw he'd snagged my attention. "She said she always buys a new plant for the spring season and sets it out around the beginning of May. She prefers geraniums because they bloom all season and don't get finicky about watering. In fact, they like a little neglect, Miz Lowery says. Just snip off the dead leaves and flowers and pop! Out come more buds, sure as you're born."

I pushed past the gardening tips as I drained the first can of Miller Lite. "What made her worried in June? About the flowers, I mean."

"Miz Lowery said she always keeps the flowerpot on the right side of her door. That way her neighbor, Mr. Madison, can enjoy the pretty color from his front window. Way I see it, she's got her flirt going on."

My eyeroll was slow and my drawl even slower: "Silver foxes in heat."

"None of my business how two old fools pass the time. Miz Lowery has a right to her fun." Norment shrugged. He was pushing sixty-nine, but he didn't see his vigor mirrored in these old-folks' antics. "Never fail, she says, she always puts the geraniums on the right side of the door. But then one morning four weeks ago, when she comes to grab the newspaper, she saw the flowerpot had trundled itself to the left side of the door. Well, she wrestled it over to its proper place on the right side. And there it hunkered. Until four mornings later, out she pops to pick up the paper. And whoops! The flowers have jumped again. Back to the left side."

Norment's shaggy dog story was growing into a hairy geranium tale. I threw some questions to show I was tracking his account. "Mrs. Lowery never saw someone move the pot? Nobody ever say they'd pushed the flowers around to get them more sunlight?"

"Nah, none of that."

"No noises at night? No barking dogs or whining cats or scraping cement?"

"Nothing. She sleeps on the third floor, so she's not right on top of the porch. And she is pushing seventy-six, so her hearing's not the sharpest. But no, she swears she didn't hear nothing. Not a peep from those flowers. They just up and moved themselves from one side of the front stoop to the other on little ghost feet."

"So, this is the Case of the Night-Creeping Geraniums?" I grinned around a deep slug of beer.

Norment ignored my sneering tone and rolled on with his account of the mysterious facts. "And then, you got to figure into it the weight of the pot. That wasn't some plastic container painted to look like cement. It's the real deal. I tried lifting it myself. I could do it, but it took some effort. It got so Miz Lowery decided if the flowers wanted to wander, she wasn't going to fight with 'em. So, she bought one of those little plastic trays with wheels and she put that under the damn sneaky pot. So now when the flowers get a mind to traipse to the other side of the porch, she can haul them to where they belong without straining her back."

I stroked my chin, then wiped wet fingers on my shirt front. "Makes sense. It's nature sending a message, Norment: Let the flowers run free." I was born too late for the Summer of Love, but I could still endorse the old hippie sentiment.

We took deep swigs from our cans. I hadn't been talking much, so I finished my beer first and crumpled the aluminum. To let Norment catch up, I dangled another string of questions. "How often does this happen? Do the flowers waltz on a regular schedule? Or is it random?"

"Miz Lowery says the pot moves at least once a week, most often on Thursday nights. Sometimes twice a week, Sunday and Thursday nights." Norment eyed my second can of beer. "You got any ideas? What you figure is going on?"

I popped the top, took a good gulp, then ran the perspiring aluminum over my forehead. "I think it could be some kind of signal."

"How do you mean *signal*?" Tension curled through Norment's twang. He'd hooked me and now he wanted me to work the case.

I drawled, letting my idea blossom as the words bubbled to the surface. "You remember in Watergate, when the secret informant Deep Throat wanted to let the reporters know he had new intel, he'd set out a flowerpot on his balcony." The more I talked, the more confident I became. "When they saw the flowers, they knew to go to their pre-arranged meeting spot."

Norment nodded in solemn remembrance of the presidential scandal, then reached for another beer. He swallowed a third of the can, then for encouragement, waved it at me.

I rolled out the explanation. "This is the same idea. Somebody is telling a partner when and where to meet by moving Mrs. Lowery's geraniums."

"Who would do such a thing?" Norment's frown suggested he understood the Nixon reference but doubted the relevance.

"Somebody who doesn't want to use a text message or phone call to reach his contact. Somebody who thinks his phone is bugged." I spread my fingers to show that the possibilities for crooked dealing were endless. "Maybe somebody who knows his wife or girlfriend is looking over his shoulder. Or somebody who wants to get the word to a crowd of people at one time."

"Yeah, could be that. And whatever the reason, you can bet your baby's milk money the content of the message is on the shady side of the law." Norment liked where I was heading and pushed new scenarios with gusto. "It might not be all the way to full-blown illegal. Maybe some player wants to hook up with his side chick and he's letting her know the coast is clear."

"Sure. It could be as simple as some down-low Romeo dogging for action. No way to confirm until we see first-hand. We have to wait for Deep Throat. Let's see who moves Mrs. Lowery's flowerpot tonight."

Hypothesis outlined and action plan fixed, we settled into a companionable silence. The afternoon's dusty haze coated the block while the Miller Lite dribbled down our throats.

As the sun flamed out, going-home traffic beat a sluggish rhythm on the street.

Sweaty office workers strolled from the subway with shirttails loose and unfurled ties draped around their necks. Nurses trudged on thick-soled clogs, leaning forward as if in perpetual climb up a steep hill. Kids exiled to the special hell of summer school lugged book bags over their shoulders. Pretty girls in drab hotel uniforms scurried toward dates, so eager to put on nighttime sparkle they started unpinning their hair as they went. No one cast a glance at the bright red geraniums.

At six, Mrs. Lowery shuffled into view, dragging a metal shopping cart to the foot of her stairs. Lime-green pants and a loose top covered with orange and lemon slices complimented her short white Afro and teak brown skin. I started to hop out to help her with the two grocery bags, but Norment gripped my forearm and shook his head. He had instructed his client to not look our way if she saw us during the stake-out and she played her part with airy confidence. She side-checked us once, raised a penciled eyebrow, then hoisted the cart up each step in slow motion.

Thirty minutes later, a handsome old gentleman, chestnut skin shiny with the weight of the day, crept up the stairs of the house next to Mrs. Lowery's. He looked sharp in a straw-colored shirt and gray slacks with wicked knife pleats. Polished two-toned Oxford shoes completed his outfit. Mrs. Lowery had set her sights on the block's slickest player. He fumbled, then dropped, a large ring of keys. He looked behind him for any witnesses to his unsteady hand and dim eye. Our car was at the curb in front of his door, but we stayed motionless, so he didn't spot us.

This was the Mr. Madison for whom Mrs. Lowery took such care with the placement of her geraniums. My guess was confirmed when the old man entered his house and turned on the overhead light in the front parlor. He took a seat in the window overlooking the street and angled his body so he faced the flowery offering without craning his neck. Mr. Madison stayed in that chair for ninety minutes, raising his arm for an occasional sip from a tall glass filled with ice and brown drink. Maybe tea; I hoped it was rum and coke. When the sun set, he pulled the shade and retreated for the night. This neighborly flirtation was dialed to a low simmer: the pilot light was still on, the juices barely sizzling.

As dusk overtook the street, cars rolled by, but from my slumped position I caught only a fleeting glimpse of the drivers. I wasn't interested in car traffic. Whoever moved the red geraniums had to approach the porch on foot. After the message was set, passing vehicles might be more important. Whoever was supposed to receive the signal wouldn't bother to amble down the block. A quick look from a car in flight would be enough to get the message.

Norment kept a steady patter through three rounds of beers. He talked about his recent cases, the romantic fortunes of his favorite TV stars, a new recipe for egg drop soup that our landlady Mei Young had tested on him, and the brutal decline of both New York baseball teams. Norment was a self-regulating engine: I didn't have to do anything more than nod in agreement and hum in amazement to keep him whirring along.

We were too far from a streetlamp for me to read my watch. But the queasy blue glow of Norment's time piece showed eight fifty-five when a shadow flowed up the stairs to Mrs. Lowery's front door. The figure was slight, wiry, and tense as a greyhound. Unlike other pedestrians, this person wore black clothing that revealed only pale palms. The skin of his scalp, face, and hands was as somber as his outfit. Sweat darkened a red bandanna twisted around his neck. He gripped the flowerpot. This was our Deep Throat.

With shoving, a twist, and a final push, he moved the geraniums to the left side of the stoop. Then he straightened to assess the placement of the pot. Too close to the door, so he pulled it forward to the lip of the porch. He stood again, this time on a lower step which dipped him into the revealing wash of lamplight.

The slack outline of a bag hung from one shoulder. The backpack was green, decorated with black lightning bolts. The same as the ones carried in the park by Whip and my dead friend Zaire. Identical to the bag I'd spotted in the tramp's hoard yesterday. Three kids holding the same backpack. A fluke too brassy to ignore. I didn't believe in coincidences; they were bad for the detective business. Run against too many accidents without connection and I'd be out of a job. Either this signal wrangler or his backpack held a clue I needed to find Zaire's killer.

CHAPTER
FOUR

Sinister backpacks bloomed all over this case. Whip's backpack had been heavy and thick; Zaire's had been empty. This signal master's satchel was deflated too. But its colors and insignia matched those of the other kids.

Satisfied with his rearrangement of the flowers, the thin boy skipped down the stairs and trotted toward the corner, flashing through alternating pools of dark and light until he dropped from sight. In that stark moment, this shaggy flower story morphed into a vital element in my case.

I tried to squeeze the triumph from my voice, but it seeped in anyway. "That's the code talker. Now we wait to see who drives by to scope the message."

Norment mumbled agreement and swiveled his head to scan the street. Maybe he caught the hitch in my breath, maybe a tic at the corner of my eye. Whatever my tell, his next question was direct.

"You see something spooked you up there?" Norment was as shrewd as they come, never missing a clue, never hesitating to probe for a lead.

Direct questions demand a direct answer. No hedges or shading allowed. Truth, as far as I knew it. Sharing my scanty information might help, even if all I had was a web of guesses. "Yes. That kid had a backpack matching one carried by the boy we saw shot dead in the park last night. I don't have proof yet, but I'll bet my next paycheck the two kids are connected somehow."

"You don't make near enough for me to take you up on that bet." Norment screwed a corner of his mouth to deliver the dig. "But your instincts is always on point. What do we do next? Follow the little signal chief, or hang here and see who comes by?"

"Stay and keep close watch on who's in his crew." I pretended more surveillance in the car was the best course of action. My hike the previous night had thrown a serious hurt on my bum foot. Showing weakness in front of the boss was never a good idea. Especially since I was hired to be the muscle of the Ross Agency. If Norment and Brina decided I wasn't up to the job, they could toss me on a moment's notice. I couldn't afford that blow to my wallet or my ego. I'd get into fighting shape with another day of rest.

"Right move, Junior. Stakeout continues. Now pass me another Miller before my tongue shrivels up like last year's shed snakeskin."

Over the next forty minutes, eleven cars passed our location. Nine of them slowed to a crawl or stopped in front of Mrs. Lowery's house. On three white index cards from a stack Norment kept in the glove compartment, I jotted the license plate number and a brief description of each vehicle. I didn't plan to share this information with the police yet, but it might come in handy sometime. Neither the skinny flowerpot wrangler nor these cruising cars had committed a crime yet. At least, not one I knew about. I'd be ready when they did.

By nine forty-five, the motor parade ended. We waited twenty minutes more. No vehicles invaded the silent street. The message hidden in Mrs. Lowery's geraniums must have been transmitted to all who cared to learn it.

"How will you report this to Mrs. L?" Beer sloshed in my mind, and I needed to take a leak. Maybe asking about the report would encourage Norment to head for home. But we'd leave when he said to and not before.

"I'll give her a skeleton write up. Times we arrived and left, who we saw move the pot, what he looked like in general terms. I'll tell her it's some kind of juvenile delinquent prank."

"Like a punk hazing ritual. Nothing more." I kept my reply short, hoping to move this stakeout to its end.

"Right. I'll leave out your ideas about the green backpack. You don't have more than a half-baked hunch anyway. No need to get her riled without more to go on. And I'll tell her we can come back next Sunday night to see if it happens again."

"Sounds good. Case wrapped. Mystery of the wandering geraniums solved." My conclusion was far too cheerful. The case of green backpacks and red flowers wasn't closed. Not by a long shot. Norment might have shared my skepticism, the flight of eyebrows toward his bald crown suggested as much. But he didn't say anything more.

Before Norment could ask, I slunk from the Taurus and muscled Mrs. Lowery's flower pot to its original place beside her door. Her vigilant suitor, Mr. Madison, could get his flirt on uninterrupted. Maybe I was a romantic after all.

Coincidences chapped my britches, but I'd risk all on a good hunch. The skinny geranium jockey had a nearby hideout. No idea for sure, but I knew where to start the search. To track him, I asked Norment to drop me at the Palace.

CHAPTER
FIVE

I tapped a speedy salute to the Pallas goddess as I entered the building. A lilac-colored puff rose from her painted breast, drifting in the moonlight. I hoped she'd forgive my next move; I wasn't the first man to piss in that doorway, the urine stench was strong, reducing my guilt. Still, I wanted divine favor on my side. So, I patted her chest again before I hit the stairs.

At the far end of the great hall, four figures crouched on their haunches around a fire built in the lid of a garbage pail. Flames danced orange and yellow before their pinched faces, casting shadows over their slender bodies. Bulging outlines of the satchels on their backs made them look like hunched gargoyles. Their mouths gaped in pleasure, laughter defeating the dark.

The backpacks gave them military flair, like a rogue army unit on maneuvers. Did these roving teenagers prefer backpacks because they refused to pile their belongings into shopping carts or trash bags the way older vagrants did? These kids owned style. Street cool. They flaunted membership in hip culture with these green-and-black backpacks. Hats, neck chains, shirts, sneakers, or backpacks. Showing off dope accessories established their cherished tribal affiliation.

When the four boys stood, I spotted my quarry. The flowerpot wrangler was taller than the others; the red bandanna at his neck marked him like army chevrons. I crossed the warehouse, threading through clusters of idle men until I reached my target. I wedged between two junior gangbangers, one with three rows of silver chains around his neck, the other with a blue headband above his eyebrow and a phony gold stud in his nose.

I didn't have a solid opening line, so I tossed a stale one: "You fellas come here often?"

"Who's asking?" A logical response from the third boy, a white kid whose spaghetti-blond hair slanted across a pimpled forehead. "You the cops?"

The second time in as many days I'd been tagged with police credentials. I deserved a percentage for official representation. "No. And I'm not carrying either." I raised my arms to cement the offer. "Check. If you dare." No one took the bid.

The hood with the red bandanna stepped into my personal space. "Whatchu want, then?" Up close, he looked older than the others, maybe twenty or twenty-two. His brown skin was roughened by clumsy razor strikes against his scant beard. Under the bandanna, a crude tattoo of blue hearts and blood-soaked razorblades decorated his neck.

"I'm looking for a kid." I delivered the truth. Direct question earned direct answer.

"Chicken hawk looking for a kid to pluck!" The chorus flapped fingers in obscene gestures then grabbed their crotches. Shrill laughter rose over barnyard noises. "Bawk-bawk, bawk-bawk, chicken hawk!"

Snickers from the troops dwindled when Red Bandanna broke through the screeching. "What kind you like, gimp? Boys, girls, something in-between? You gotta get specific for us to hook you up with the right chicken."

"Specific." The chorus echoed, "Yeah, get specific, chicken hawk."

"His name is Whip." I addressed Red Bandanna; no need to waste breath on the others. "You know him."

"Know him? Why would I know him?" Sparse eyebrows bent together as his mouth twisted in scorn.

"You carry the same green backpack he does."

Air rushed in harsh bursts from three boys, but they remained silent, waiting for their leader to respond. "Yeah, what if I do?"

"He's a friend of Zaire's." I swung my hunch like a pickaxe. "You know him too, right?"

The blond kid piped to his chief, "Why he asking us about that mess for, Link?"

The tall boy dipped his chin, cutting his eyes to the right. Two of his crew stepped to my flanks, digging bony fingers into my elbows. "You got all kinds of specific ideas about us, gimp. Too specific."

Silver chains jingled as their owner twisted my left arm then jerked the hand toward the shoulder blade. The boy with the blue sweatband wrenched my right thumb and pressed it into the small of my back. I relaxed my shoulders; I wanted answers, not fisticuffs.

Link stepped closer, his tobacco-drenched breath smearing my face. He was two inches shorter and fifty pounds lighter than me. Hard and straight like iron rebar. Dark eyes, flat as tarnished dimes, shimmered between narrowed lids. He ran two fingers over scarce black whiskers on his chin. Shoulder twitched; elbow jutted. The tip of a switchblade bit skin at my throat. "Give me a name, old man. If I like it, I might let you go with just a scratch. Or two." He nudged the knife towards my Adam's apple.

"Rook."

Link stroked the knife down my shirt placket, slipping the blade under the first button. "What kinda name is that?" He flicked and the button popped into the air. "Some kinda superhero street handle?" Sniggers tickled my ears from both sides.

"The name my father gave me." The blond kid hooted at my claim, but I kept eyes on the chief. "Tell me what I want to know, and I'll leave you in one piece. Link."

"Bold." The thin boy lowered his voice. "You awful bold for a trapped man with a crip leg."

"Link. What's that short for anyway? *Chain* Link? *Missing* Link?"

He sliced two more buttons from my shirt. The white disks scurried like roaches across the wooden floor. When Link nodded, the hoods behind me jammed my arms again. Pain darted from shoulders to groin. The shirtfront gaped, sweat streaking dark on my undershirt. Link flicked the knife again, the gash in the damp fabric left my skin exposed but intact.

He pressed the blade behind my left ear, drawing it toward my jaw. Spittle sprayed over my right cheek as Link's stooge spoke: "Whatchu gonna do to him, Link? Like you done to that calico kitten last week?"

Fire threaded through my flesh as blood dribbled past my collarbone. Link chuckled. "He don't need *two* ears, do he? Any more than that fucking cat did."

A crooked shadow rushed past my right shoulder. "Drop it, boy." The words grated over a deep rumble. "You break the peace of this camp again, you gonna pay a high price."

Eddie the Pauper jammed his huge head between my ribs and Link's blade. "You been warned, boy. I had enough of you tonight. Pack it up."

Link slipped the knife into his pocket and retreated a step. "You protecting nasty perverts like this now? What the fuck's up with you, Eddie?"

"You puzzle too hard about it, your head like to explode." Eddie squared on the skinny kid. "You ain't got the brain power, boy. So, beat it."

Link thrust his jaw to the left and slanted his eyes in the same direction. The punks behind me released my arms. As I hitched shoulders to restore circulation, the four hoods melted into the gloom near the entrance to the great hall.

"Thanks, Eddie." I shrugged to ease the numbness. "It's good to see you again."

"You *better* thank me, fool. You worked yourself into a pretty fix. I seen you when you first come in. Watched to see how'd you do. You misjudged them, Rook. Let those cheap no-account thugs get the jump on you."

The old man dug a purple plaid handkerchief from his coat pocket and tossed it at my face. I dabbed the crumpled cloth against my ear to staunch the bleeding. Eddie gulped a lungful, then dumped on me. "Them's rough boys. I seen Whip talking with 'em too. And now you.

Don't mess with them punks, they nothing but danger. I can't protect but so far. The disaster them gangbangers bring is beyond my reach. I told Whip that. And now I'm warning you."

I ducked my head at the scolding. Then switched subjects: "You seen Whip around?"

"When I do, I'll tell you." The milky cast of Eddie's brown eyes froze. "And when he's ready to see you, he'll find you. Count on it."

Stung and frustrated, I turned for the exit. Eddie shuffled beside me, weaving a crooked path around packing crates and dented metal chairs at the edge of the vast room. When we got to the door, I tossed another question. "Your threat to Link and his crew. How'd you make it stick?"

Eddie tilted his bushy head toward three figures lounging before an arched window. "You see them men over there?" Silhouetted against the purple-streaked sky, their faces were obscured. But the outline of chiseled muscles and pit-bull necks stood clear.

"What about them?"

"I did for them, now they do for me. They owe me. And they pay their debts in power."

"You did them favors?"

"You see that brother with the ripped sleeves and black eye patch? Khalif. A year ago, he fell into the butt end of a fight. His prize was a split right eyeball and four teeth missing. Would a choked on his own vomit if I hadn't reached into his mouth and pulled those teeth out his throat. Now Khalif owes me."

"Same with the others?"

"Same. They enforce for me." Eddie flashed his first smile of the evening. "Rulers comes in all shapes and sizes, Rook. Those punks with the green satchels know it. Now, so do you."

I offered my hand. After we shook, Eddie pointed a jagged yellow nail at my undershirt. "Men used to call them 'wife-beaters.'" I fingered the rip in the sweat-stained cloth as he continued: "I always hated that nasty name."

Blazing eyes and clinched fists hinted at an untold story. I raised my brows, hoping he'd elaborate, but the hobo turned his back. The hem of his wool overcoat dragged trails through the dust as he retreated toward his mattress. School was closed for the evening. On my way out, I dropped a tender pat on the goddess's painted toga: she'd delivered. I had a name for my hunch, "Link." And another connection to the homeless camp. As I slogged through the humid night, Eddie's lessons nipped at the hunches playing ring-a-rosy in my mind.

CHAPTER
SIX

Though he had said he'd write the report on the flowery Lowery case, Norment assigned me the drudge work the next morning. Drafting it took thirty minutes. I spent the rest of the afternoon amending it to Norment's specifications. Which was fine, as the summer heat had burned our workload to ashes.

Waiting for Norment to comb through my report for the fourth time, I pulled a pad of yellow legal paper from my desk drawer to make a pencil sketch of Mrs. Lowery's front step. I tore off that sheet and folded it into a jet airplane, landing it in the waste basket near the coat rack. Then I put the paper to better use. I wrote an eight-sentence profile of the shadowy figure I'd seen on the porch. "Link" went at the top of the page in block letters. His muscled chest and slender waist put him in his early twenties. The heft of the pot said he was strong and motivated. Was he driven by duty or fear? Black jeans and black long-sleeved shirt said he wasn't beaten by the heat or influenced by casual fashion. He carried the same backpack as other members of his crew, but he'd added a red bandanna as a style note, asserting his individuality. His stealthy posture and close attention to placement of the geranium pot meant his job was serious. Was he a general or a raw recruit in this weighty mission? How was the code talker related to Whip and the sacrificed Zaire? I stuffed the yellow sheet of musings into the center drawer of my desk.

That evening I strolled to the street bordering the homeless camp where I'd last seen Whip. I'd left my message and my card, but spying cost nothing. Despite Eddie's warning, if I spotted the kid, I'd force the contact. I claimed the second step on a shadowed cement stoop opposite the Palace entrance. After staring at me through the traffic for five minutes, two younger men joined me on the landing. They frowned at my invasion, but I played dumb, dipping a head-bob to keep the peace. One man was dressed in denim overalls covering bare skin, like a rogue cowboy. The rural look was vetoed by the knit cap in red, black, green, and yellow stretched over his Rasta dreads. His pointy-nosed boots had tall underslung heels. Genuine western working boots, like the pair I'd left in my mother's attic in San Marcos. His partner wore red nylon shorts drooping to his skinny calves and a stained white t-shirt under a green warm-up jacket. He was growing his hair, but had a long way to go before those puny knots achieved his pal's epic dreadlocks.

I hadn't smoked since army days, but lounging in public looked better with a cigarette. Tobacco made me seem sociable rather than idle, less threatening. More brother than snitch. More neighbor than narc. Marlboros worked as a prop for surveillance. I opened my dented pack and offered a cigarette to each neighbor. The smokes were accepted with a nod, but not lit: the fellas had better things to do with a match than light my tobacco. As soon as he'd stowed my cigarette in his bib pocket, the cowboy–he introduced himself as Tills—pulled out a blunt as thick as his thumb and fired its tight-rolled tip. The other guy, Morris, sucked a mighty gale, then thrust the joint in my direction.

The next forty minutes evaporated in happy silence, the joint passing between us like a peace pipe. I limited my blow to every other round; I wanted to stay alert, without rejecting the generosity of my new best friends. I was a cheap date; Tills and Morris didn't object to economizing. My contact high was mostly smog, humid but powerful all the same. Sweet and smoky, the weed tasted like caramelized onions. And smelled like the underside of a beautiful woman's arm when she's skipped shaving for a week. Musk crossed with syrup, sexy and magical like that.

The dope was so powerful, if Odette had cruised along the pavement on the other side of the street, I might have missed her in the ganja haze. But she pushed her shopping cart right below the stoop where we lounged. Odette looked free and aimless, ambling at a Sunday pace. I hauled myself down the stairs and only stumbled once as I trotted after her. She was so slow I caught up before she reached the corner.

"Odette, remember me?" I passed my hand over my face to whisk away the Maryjane cloud.

"Sure, honey! You and your cousin Thurman are hard to forget. Those crazy beautiful eyes you boys flash are enough to make an old woman wish for younger days."

I wondered again about her fixation on my nonexistent cousin. Who was this mysterious "Thurman" haunting her imagination? Through the dope haze, I tried to focus on a mole over her left eyebrow, but it jumped like a sizzling corn kernel on a skillet. She blinked once, then again, bringing my face into definition as her pupils narrowed.

Two corks on an ocean swell, we bobbed in the wake of our personal highs. We might have floated there all evening, smiling and stoned. But I remembered I wanted something from her. Something big. If only I could drag it through the soupy fog. "It's good to see you too, Odette."

She crumpled her hands in the folds of her long skirt. Her elegant fingers made graceful pleats in the fabric, a frothy drape of purple and gold, perfect curtains for a Paris brothel. Her turn to talk. Instead, she lifted the top layer of netting and pressed it over her mouth. Hiding the lower half of her face enhanced the almond shape of her dark eyes as she winked at me.

When she offered only an admiring stare, I plunged on before she burst into a torch song. The fog shifted and that big something I wanted to ask about shimmered into view. "I was hoping I'd hear from Whip this week."

"What you want with that kid?" Disappointment then scorn shimmied across her features.

"Like I told you and Eddie, I think Whip needs help."

"Nothing but trouble, that's Whip. Nothing but a plague. If you smart, you stay away from that kid. I told Eddie. But he never listens. What you say your name was again?" Odette dropped the drapery from her face, revealing a turned down pout.

To duck her fierce gaze, I glanced at the grocery cart she'd been pushing. It was filled with neat stacks of cloth. Stray scraps, detached sleeves, frayed collars, or vagrant pockets that must have been tailored clothing in a past life. Ghost of dresses, men's trousers, blouses, and overcoats cluttered the colorful assortment. Odette also collected paper. She'd saved bales of newsprint, posters, flyers, letters, coupons, even squares of aluminum foil. Folded flat, under a tall pile of Vogue magazines, was a black-and-green backpack. The prize, the connection, the Mayan treasure at the end of my jungle expedition. The clue.

Electricity charged through the weedy fog. But she'd asked a question, so I stuck with the basics: "My name's Rook." She nodded, murky recognition surfing over her face. Maybe another round of disappointment too. Afraid of losing her altogether, I pressed. "Odette, can I take a look in your cart?" I tilted my head to stretch my flirtation muscles.

"Nobody touches my things! Didn't your momma teach you never go grabbing in a lady's purse. It's rude." She clamped thin fingers on the push-bar of the grocery cart and spat her words with defiance.

I lowered my speech to a dopey purr. In high school this voice worked magic once or twice, maybe the charm lingered. "I won't disturb anything. Just a look, that's all."

"Look at what, honey?" She was in seduction mode again.

"That green satchel there." I pointed through the metal grate at the backpack.

Odette leaned over the cart, ruffling her long fingers through the treasure like a reference librarian searching for a document. She tugged the backpack, lifting the magazines until it was freed. She presented the bag to me on trembling hands. "This what you want, baby?"

"Yes." I extended my fingers, but Odette wrapped the backpack in long arms and pressed it to her chest. "What you gonna give me for it?" When I looked stupid, she pointed at my belly button and offered a suggestion. "Give me that pretty leather belt you got on. With the

Sleeping Beauty turquoise stone in the silver clasp. Mighty fine. I'll take that."

I traced a finger across the graceful carvings of the buckle. The nugget was the size of my pinkie fingernail and as clear as a summer sky at dawn. No way could I give it up. "Odette, this belt was a gift from my mother. For high school graduation. I can't trade it."

She stared at my waist for thirty seconds. I shifted from one foot to the other. My jeans felt hot, my sneakers itchy and tight. She stared for another twenty beats until I wanted to rip the t-shirt from my chest.

Then she sighed, acknowledging a universal truth. "No, you better not give away nothing you got from your momma. It's bad luck." She handed me the backpack with a gummy grin, the trade forgotten.

"Thank you, Odette."

I checked first for bullet holes. If this backpack belonged to Zaire, it might have been damaged in the hail of bullets that killed him. It was unmarked. Maybe Whip had used it. This backpack was identical to the one worn by the code talker Link when I'd seen him dragging the pot of geraniums. I thrust a hand inside, scrabbling for clues which might reveal who'd owned it. I found a fistful of red rubber bands, shredded and torn. The loose ball looked like a nest of earthworms; the elastics seemed to writhe as they lay in my palm.

I stared so long, Odette wondered at my intense interest. "Baby, you want them things? You take 'em. I don't collect no rubber bands. Especially not broken ones. You keep 'em, if you want."

I pocketed the clutch of rubber. Maybe sense would emerge from the spongy tangle later on. Once the dope wore off. "Thank you, Odette. I appreciate it."

She took the backpack and slotted it into the stack at the exact place from where she'd taken it, a card slipped into a catalog file drawer. When she'd secured her collection, Odette stroked a long hand over a brocade scrap and looked at me.

"You think all this here is trash, don't you? But I'll tell you something special. Look at me now and you might not believe it, but back in the day, when you were just a pretty puppy, Odette was the most sought-after fit model on Seventh Avenue. They said Odette's body was perfect, a perfect size four. Every fashion house used Odette's body to build their empire. Every one of 'em needed me. Odette was an industry princess, high fashion royalty."

She sighed and gazed at the passing traffic. Thick liquid, like rubber cement glue, leaked from the corner of her right eye.

"Things went around. Then came around. Like a revolving door. I was in fashion, then out of fashion. In style, out of style. But the coke never quit, did it? Nasty old daddy coke kept after Odette until he got her good. Now I'm out here collecting the fashion I used to wear. Saving it from the trash. They call it 'haute couture.' You ever heard of that?"

She swung her glance toward me again, its sharpness falling like a pickaxe across my face. "High fashion. It's high alright, that's for sure. But, drugs or no, I still got an eye for cut and texture. This isn't garbage I got in here. Some bold experiments right in here. Best believe it, honey. So, don't say Odette never gave you nothing. Right?"

"Right, I won't." My cheek tingled with warmth as I dragged my hand over the stubble.

She turned with a flounce, long skirts lifting from skinny ankles. Crossing the street to the warehouse, Odette pushed her cart around a white van that slowed to let her pass. When she reached the warehouse entrance, she paused next to the grimy painting of the Greek goddess. Through the exhaust fumes of the van, Odette threw a wink over her shoulder. I caught it and winked back.

CHAPTER
SEVEN

The jellybean-pink sandal zipped past my ear. I snatched it with my left hand then grabbed the collar of the pitcher with my right fist. She struggled but I subdued the ten-year-old culprit with minimal fuss.

This cousin-on-cousin violence was the highlight of the Garland family gathering Saturday evening. We'd been hired to provide security for the roof-top party. Such venues are generally rich with family tension and neighborly unrest. But an overdose of goodwill bogged down the party: the music was tedious, the dancing cloddish, and the flirting amateur. Despite Grandma Garland's fears, the family factions didn't break into open warfare over drug turf. Not even a wig or hoop earring was snatched the whole night.

With or without the neighborhood's finest weed, my hours slogged on in a humid daze. The Ross Agency was stuck in mid-summer doldrums. No one knocked on our door with worries about a lost child or paycheck or fiancé or dog.

Waiting for Whip to contact me was fraying my nerves. Had Eddie the Pauper given the boy my card? Did Whip tear it to shreds? Had he laughed at my do-gooder concern? Maybe Whip had decided I was nosy or crazy or perverted or all of the above. If I didn't hear from the kid by the end of the day, I'd visit the homeless camp again to force a break in the case.

Waiting for Brina to confirm our personal situation was taxing my temper too. She was foot-dragging without explanation. Twice I asked if she'd bought a home pregnancy test kit. Twice she snapped no. When I dropped in a Duane Reade to get toothpaste, I thought of buying her a kit to push the question forward. Visions of canine teeth and severed veins danced in my head. So, I revised my idea, saved my neck, and stuck to my tube of Colgate.

Sensing the dangerous clash of boredom and panic roiling me, Brina suggested I join her on a tiny job at an establishment we both knew well, Friends In Deed. When I first arrived in New York, I'd spent many hours in the solace of this Quaker settlement house on the border of our neighborhood and Spanish Harlem. In addition to a soup kitchen which fed hundreds each day, the Friends In Deed dormitory provided housing for men, and for women and their children. A clothing depot distributed shirts, pants, and toiletries to homeless people, while a training program offered basic business skills to strivers of every condition and prospect.

As Brina and I walked through the hushed space of the old deconsecrated church, I remembered many nights I'd come to this place craving a hot meal, a warm bed, or a calm word of advice. The mild souls of Friends In Deed had saved my life. If I solved a puzzle or unraveled a mystery for them now, I'd knock a few pennies from the huge debt I owed.

"I thought there'd be more people at this hour. For dinner." Brina's voice piped softly at my shoulder.

I glanced at the few stragglers hanging on the benches beside tables that stretched down the nave. "They serve dinner early, five to six."

"Why so early? What's the rush?"

"People are hungry. And anxious to get wherever they're going to spend the night. People appreciate the early meal and the chance to get settled before the sun goes down."

"Makes sense." She peered toward the rear of the room, looking for familiar faces. Brina mentioned she'd been contacted by Keisha Reynolds, one of the center's associate directors. "I thought Keisha might be here to greet us."

"Busy in the kitchen, maybe. She supervises clean up, doesn't she?"

Nodding, Brina stepped around the last table. She wiped the back of her hand over her brow, leaving a streak of dust in the sweat. I handed her a balled tissue from my pocket and gestured at her forehead.

She patted the skin before continuing. "Yeah, she sounded anxious to see us. But reluctant too. Like she was bursting with questions, but hesitant to give more than a skeletal description."

"Something's troubling her. She'll fill in the details."

We pushed through the swinging doors at the rear of the great hall. The kitchen of Friends In Deed was impressive despite its simplicity. The double height ceiling dwarfed plain fixtures: twin white refrigerators, a deep farm sink with an apron of white enamel, long rows of upper cabinets painted dove gray. Although the white subway tiles lining the backsplash were cracked in places, the enormous stainless-steel range looked brand new. Maybe some rich supporter had made the donation; the appliance looked too fancy for the humble staff of Friends In Deed to have picked it on their own. The lower cabinets around the room were fire engine red, a color repeated on the island that dominated the center of the space.

When Brina and I arrived at the kitchen, Keisha and her boss, Sondra Crane, executive director of Friends In Deed, were bent over a cardboard box on the island's stainless steel countertop. The two women, similar in age, were opposites in every other aspect. Keisha was short and round, her curves straining the khaki pantsuit above and below the waist. Dr. Crane wrapped her slender body in a bright orange cardigan over a flowered dress buttoned to the neck despite the summer heat. Both women wore their hair in elaborate braided styles that swirled across their heads.

Together the pair raised their eyes as we entered. We were on time for our appointment, so neither seemed surprised to see us; maybe they preferred the informal setting of the kitchen. Keisha beckoned with a smile and a fluttering hand gesture. "Thanks for coming out in this heat. Can we get you something cool from the fridge? Iced tea or water?"

I started to decline, but Brina said yes to the tea. In a flash, two tumblers and a sweating glass pitcher appeared on the island counter.

"I know you remember Dr. Sondra from the last time you visited, Mr. Rook. I'm so glad you decided to come with Brina. I don't know if you all can help us, but I told Dr. Sondra that if anyone could solve our little problem, it would be the Ross Agency."

I tossed a mock frown at the two. "If we're going to work together, ladies, you have to call me Rook. *Mister* Rook is my father." Long gone and unlamented, Sheldon Rook still deserved the title.

Neither Keisha nor Sondra acted as if they recognized me from the bad old days. I'd visited Friends In Deed on a regular basis back then. But I'd changed since those gutter-bound times two years ago. Maybe the clean shave and close hair cut really did change my look. Shaggy Old Testament-style coils and beard made me one of those filthy prophets you didn't want sleeping on your front step. Or maybe it was the pressed slacks and fresh white shirt. Or the few pounds regular eating put on my frame. I was still lean, but not scarecrow spindly anymore. Maybe Quaker restraint kept Keisha and Sondra from mentioning my dismal time on the streets. No matter the reason, I was grateful for their discretion. Brina knew the outline of my rough past; I'd kept it a secret from her in a sad ploy that had threatened our relationship. Revelation had cleared the air three months ago, but I wanted to avoid delving further. If the Quaker ladies intended to keep quiet, so would I.

Sondra Crane squeezed my hand with a hearty pump then thrust a glass into it. Though her smile was broad, the tension that bubbled in her dark brown eyes made the hairs on my neck rise. "Rook, it is. I hope you're right, Keisha. This problem's like a knot worrying the back of my throat. I can't swallow right until I get it untied. Can you pull up those pictures we wanted Brina to look at?"

The women had been examining the contents of a shoebox when we came in, but they turned our attention to a cell phone on the counter between them. Keisha thumbed through a gallery of photos until she came to the ones she wanted.

The first photo was tinted purple. A human ear dominated the left side of the image. In the background was the glassed frame of a shelter for a bank's automatic teller machine. The sidewalk in front of the ATM was covered in lilac grass clippings, the sky was colored deep lavender. The ear was dark, though curlicues sprang toward the hidden cheekbone. The hair was violet, probably black rinsed by a purple filter. The lobe had a tiny mark where an earring might have been but no other scars.

"When did you get this picture, Dr. Sondra?" Brina turned the phone at an angle as she studied the odd image.

"This one came around five this evening. As usual, the message with it pointed us to a location around the church campus. This time it was to the broom closet on the first floor of the men's dorm."

"As *usual*?" Brina's eyes widened at the phrase which caught my attention too.

"Yes, we've received three other photos like this over the past two months. Always accompanied by a message telling us to look in a different spot. Once in a box of used clothing left at the kitchen door. Once in a tool shed in the courtyard. Once in the kitchen pantry."

I glanced at the three women, who kept their faces blank as they waited for my explanation. I had no handle on this puzzle, but I made a stab anyway. "Anonymous donor, maybe. I assume you found money there? And this is the way he wants you to know he's helping out. Like a signature. He doesn't want a thank you, but he does need to be acknowledged. Another shy retiring rich dude, that's all. How much did you find?" I lifted the corner of my mouth instead of winking, but I couldn't get the women to smile at my weak joke.

Keisha pushed the conversation forward. "Maybe, Rook. But that's not all there is to this little puzzle."

Sondra shoved the cardboard box toward me and lifted its lid. Inside were four bricks of twenty-dollar bills, each bound in a red rubber band.

"Every time a photo comes, we follow the clue and we find money wrapped up in the clothes, hidden where the message tells us to look. And the total is always the same, three thousand dollars. Exact. That's almost enough for our monthly rent here." Keisha shook her head in wonder.

The amount of cash was appalling, the mystery intriguing. One clue slipped into place: these red rubber bands matched the broken elastics I'd taken from the backpack in Odette's shopping cart. There was a connection, I was sure of it, taunting me to unwind its tangles. I pushed forward: "Same picture each time?"

The younger woman shook her head again and tapped at the phone. Pictures flashed across the shiny surface in a strange slide show. Three photos were identical to the first in color palette: purple ranging from violet to lilac rinsed over the images. But each picture was of a different part of a face, crafted into compositions that disguised the subject even as features were revealed. Selfies in purple. The liquid inner corner of an eye dominated one photo, violet depressions carved against the soft incline of the nose. Another shot made the clean curve of the jawline look as if it were cut from Mount Rushmore. The fourth picture showed a full bottom lip, its edge black and the indentation below slanting to indigo shadows.

"Is this even the same person?" Brina spoke for the first time in many minutes. "Maybe these are fractured portraits of four different people."

"You mean a band of Robin Hoods? Dressed in purple?" Cynicism curled my words.

Keisha's expression clouded at my sarcastic joke. Sondra's face was shiny with unease, but also with a wistful hope. She wanted these curious donations to belong to Friends In Deed. The money would go a long way toward keeping the modest organization afloat during the dry summer months until donations revved up in the holiday season.

I dropped the teasing: "Sondra, why haven't you spent it yet?"

"Keisha said we should wait to find out where the money came from. Who it really belongs to." As she made that plain declaration Sondra sighed, but there didn't seem to be any regret in the expression. Years of loyalty reinforced her agreement with her associate's instincts in this matter. They were allies in faith and work; they had each other's backs all the way. "We want to try to return it to its rightful owner."

Sondra's firm statement cast a silence that drifted over us until a new voice boomed in the lofty kitchen. "I been looking all over for you, Keisha. I rounded up two girls to help me with chopping the vegetables for tomorrow's lunch. Now you just got to tell me where you hid them potatoes."

A woman with a hard jaw pulled the screen door of the kitchen and barged in from the rear courtyard. She was tall, five ten or more, with long hands and feet to match. Her red-brown skin had the slick finish of a worry bead. She'd scraped her hair into a top-knot so tight it gave me a headache to look at it. She might have been forty-five; her waist and hips were thick. But the absence of makeup and the smoothness of her cheeks gave her a youthful air.

"Leola, can't you see I'm in a meeting?" Keisha didn't sound as irritated as her bare words suggested. The interruption seemed to be an expected event.

Sondra Crane stepped in with introductions, blocking whatever might remain of her colleague's annoyance. "Brina, Rook. This is Leola Covington. She stays here at the center. And lends a hand with preparing our meals most days. Leola, our guests are helping with a little problem that's got us scratching our heads these past few weeks."

The newcomer scowled, her mouth gaping in fury. "You had no call to bring in the cops, Dr. Sondra. Let me take a look see before you do a damned fool thing like that."

Brina spoke in soothing tones. "We're not cops, Leola. We're friends, trying to help if we can."

Leola gave us a once-over that scraped like Brillo pads. I didn't pass muster, earning another scouring glare. But after long study, she nodded approval of Brina.

"So, what's got you all stumped here?" Leola held out her giant hand. When Sondra placed the phone in her palm, it looked like a child's toy.

Leola's scream jolted us: "That's my Whitney! What're you doing with pictures of my baby!" The wail bounced off the steel counter. "And why you paint her face purple!"

CHAPTER
EIGHT

A mother's howl is the worst sound in the world. Piercing and weird, pitiful and righteous, a mother can knife you with her shriek.

Under the barrage of questions from the three women, Leola Covington's rising alarm pummeled me. Her eyes shrank in their sockets, breath hammering under her heavy chest. Leola had seemed strong; now she was battered and bewildered. Why didn't Keisha rush to her rescue? Why did Sondra hang back? No one offered help, letting the screams roll across the kitchen unblocked.

"That's my baby girl! Where you keeping her?" The woman's eyes darted from face to face. Her shoulders sagged, as if she'd sink to the floor in agony. "What I done to deserve this? Why you hiding her from me?"

Shaken, I tried to stop her collapse. "Leola, don't worry. You haven't done anything wrong." I rounded the island and touched her left forearm. Sondra approached from the other side, taking little steps as if confronting an uncaged lion. Leola's anxiety turned rancid in the sweat on her blouse. I squeezed her icy hand. "Tell us what you can about the person in this picture. Do you know her name?"

"Of course, I know her name! She's my daughter, Whitney. My baby. My poor, gone baby."

Leola turned her red eyes toward the director, like an exhausted runner sagging in the last yards before the finish line. "You recognize Whitney, don't you, Doctor Sondra? That's her jaw and her ear. They's just like that. Don't you see how her mouth favors me? Why you didn't tell me you had pictures of my baby? Why you keep it a secret from me?"

Sondra recoiled from the accusation of callousness. "I'm sorry. I didn't recognize Whit." Mean was not in her self-description, and the blame made her voice shake. "But now you point it out, Leola, I do see the resemblance. I'm so sorry we didn't let you know about these pictures earlier, but we just didn't make the connection. Did you, Keisha?"

Her deputy gasped, distress spilling into sweat on her nose. They were the open-hearted, all-knowing, careful ones. This lapse stung Keisha as much as it did the sorrowing mother. "Oh, no! I apologize, Leola. It never crossed my mind this could be somebody we knew."

As Leola wailed, Keisha's lips sagged open, failure crumpling the contours of her round face. She mumbled through fingers pressed to her teeth. "Leola and Whitney came to us seven months ago. They lived in our dormitory while they looked for permanent housing. Leola's been in our jobs training program learning business computer skills for six weeks now."

I feared Leola wouldn't appreciate being talked about in the third person, like she was a science experiment or a social improvement project. But the empty look on her face showed she was too far inside her own anguish to notice Keisha's words bubbling on.

"Until April, Whitney was doing real well in a city-wide high school for kids without homes. But then she dropped out of school and ran away from here too." As Keisha finished, gray lines pleated around her mouth. She looked as stricken as the sobbing mother.

Hugs from Sondra and wads of paper towels pressed against her face muffled Leola's cries. Standing next to her, a useless dolt without a purpose, I patted her arm until the noise dwindled to snuffling moans.

Brina cut her eyes toward the door, hinting we should go and let the women be miserable without us. But I slid my jaw sideways and mouthed a silent "no." Questions swirled in my head, vague hints forming into hunches. The ideas weren't solid yet, just jelly-like flesh without bones to support them. But something was there, grumbling to be recognized. I needed answers and I wasn't budging until I had them.

After another minute of the awful racket, Sondra raised her voice in command: "Keisha, take Leola back to her room. Help her get settled for the night. I'll finish up with Brina and Rook. We'll make a plan for how we go forward with all this."

Protest and sass shocked out of her, Leola seemed to shrink six inches under the weight of the evening's discoveries. Diminished, she was easy to shepherd through the kitchen's back door. Once the women were gone, Brina and I followed Sondra to her office in an alcove off the main dining hall. As we sat, my foot welcomed the relief and my ears were glad of the quiet. But the hard chair in front of Sondra's desk felt like the furniture in every principal's office I'd ever visited. Unfocused guilt mixed with ignorance inside me. Brina didn't help; since I'd signaled I wanted to stay, she let me take the lead. Or the ruler slaps.

Sondra got right to the point, her crisp tones reinforcing my feeling she was the disciplinarian, looking for someone to spank. "Rook, your eyes are bouncing like pinballs. You got ideas charging through your head. What do you know about this mess?"

I glanced at Brina, and then trudged on. "I don't have answers yet. But I do have new questions. You can clarify some points in what Leola and Keisha said." Enlisting Sondra's help in this investigation was the best way to push this investigation forward.

"Go ahead, then. I'll try as best I can. But you need to understand our rules. We're not priests here, but we do respect the confidentiality of our clients." Sondra paused to let the warning sink in. "They sometimes share difficult things, personal issues, with us. And we have to hold that information close to protect their privacy. I'll answer you with as much detail as I can. But there's a line I can't cross."

I accepted the caution and slotted it into my own religious background. "A confessional minus the incense and Latin chants? That's okay, Doctor Sondra." When her shoulders relaxed, I continued. "Give me what you can. First: Leola's daughter is called 'Whit?' Is that the name she goes by?"

"Yes, that's what the girl shortened it to. I guess 'Whitney' felt too fancy for her tastes."

Sondra leaned back in her chair, hands clasped in her lap. I raised my eyebrows to urge her on. "From the first day they got here, the Covingtons clashed about it: Leola used the full name 'Whitney,' but her daughter insisted on 'Whit.' They fought all the time, screaming in the dorm, shouting at the dining table. The other residents complained to me about their crying and raging. We tried to help. But despite the peace talks, they never resolved anything and then the daughter disappeared."

Sondra pinched her mouth, snipping the final words, and lowered her lashes. She dragged her fingers over her upper lip. She was withholding parts of the story. Maybe she found the specifics distasteful or forbidden. But she was censoring crucial facts. Details I needed.

I pushed for more. "What was it they argued about? The name? Whitney versus Whit? What else did they fight about? What prompted Whit to run away from her own mother? And stay away for almost five months now?"

The issue between parent and child was a tough one, touchy and personal. My impulse was to drop answers in the middle of the room, let the shrapnel hit whoever was in range of the explosion. But Sondra needed to find language that suited her. So, I shut up, waiting on her.

She inhaled, unease shrouding her open face. "You know, this isn't something I should be talking about."

"I get that. Whatever you can share will help."

"They argued about clothes."

"Clothes?"

"Whit wanted to wear pants and jeans only."

"Most kids do these days."

"But Whit wanted to wear button-down shirts, baseball caps, and baggy t-shirts only. No dresses, skirts, or blouses. Ever. They fought a lot about that."

"Anything else?"

"Whit worked chores and saved money for visits to the barber shop. For close trims and neat square shape-ups. Leola hated those tight haircuts. Hated them with the fire of a thousand suns. She used to screech and howl every time Whit came back from the barber with another low cut."

"A man's style?"

"Yes, exactly." The director sighed, wiping her hand across her lips. "It's pretty sensitive stuff, for both of them."

"Sondra, I get that. I think I may have met the kid, but I need a few more pieces of information to know for sure. I want to help. But I need to know as much as you can share."

"Well, if you really think it will help…" She shifted her head to the right, to get a better look at me.

"It will."

Sondra reached for the glass of iced tea she'd brought from the kitchen. She drained it before resuming her story. "In February, I called Whit to my office and asked about the fighting with Leola. I wanted to hear from each side in private, without the other interfering."

Sondra clasped her hands before her face, then lowered them. She'd reached resolution and plowed on with new speed. "That's when Whit told me she didn't want to be a girl anymore. She said she didn't think she ever was a girl. Not really, not deep down inside. She said she'd always felt she was a boy. She'd had these feelings since she was three or four years old, and the feelings kept getting stronger and stronger each year."

Something of the kid's determination crept into Sondra's voice as she summed up the story. "Whit said she was a boy and she always knew it."

"And that's why she wanted to change her name?"

"Yes, 'Whit' was the preferred name. And Whit wanted to use male pronouns too. She wanted us to use him instead of her, he instead of she. We kept mixing them up and she would always correct us. It wasn't just her mother who objected. Staff members and clients kept calling Whit by female pronouns too." Sondra closed her eyes. "I tried to remember. For Whit's sake. But it's hard."

The toughest part now in the open, she continued with more formality, like she was in a classroom: "Whit's a transgender person. He's consistent, persistent, and insistent on his identification as a male.

Has been for years, as far as I can tell. Whit doesn't use the term trans in self-descriptions. But at fourteen, most kids won't."

"And Leola pushed back?"

"Like a bear. She wouldn't accept it. Fought the whole idea. I thought maybe Leola was changing as the months went by. Starting to come around, but it was hard going."

The director leaned forward on her desk, her hands extended toward me, willing me to see it the same way.

I wanted to shake my head, to clear cobwebs from the shadows in the corners of my mind. But even the hint of resistance might end the story before its conclusion, so I threw another question into the silence. "But then Whit ran anyway? Why?"

Sondra sighed and ran a hand over the little beads of sweat along her hairline. "I don't know. Leola still wasn't ready to accept Whit for who he was. Her pressure was always there, sometimes subtle, but more often blatant. She nagged, she badgered, she whined. She refused to switch pronouns. The term is mis-gendering. It's applying the wrong gender to a person. Leola refused to see things the way her child did. My guess is between school, the dormitory, and the mother's complaints, it was too much for Whit. He couldn't handle the tension."

"So, in April he ran away. And you haven't heard from him since?"

"Not a peep. We called in the police, of course. But I don't think they gave a flying flip for a missing trans kid run away from a homeless shelter."

Sondra's cynical assessment was on target. For the police, it was simple: no crime, no disturbance, no rights violations, no proof of possible danger to herself or others. The cops would ditch that missing person report as soon as they learned Whit was homeless. As far as they were concerned, if the kid wasn't causing any trouble, she wasn't in any trouble. And police indifference went double for a runaway trans kid.

My hunch about the mix of identity and murder fell into place with a silent click when Sondra finished her story. I hadn't seen her up close, but the kid I followed from the park six days ago resembled Leola Covington enough to be her child. The same strong jaw, redbone skin, lanky frame, and stubborn determination. Altering the final *T* to convert the name into the cool-sounding 'Whip' seemed a probable next step in the kid's journey. The troubled Whit became the self-directed Whip with the flick of a consonant.

Telling Sondra my guesses about Whip would only cause harm. Getting her hopes raised or increasing her alarm seemed cruel. If the kid was mixed up in something illegal through involvement in the green backpack army, I'd dig into it on my own.

But I could share one guess from my mental file of clues. "Sondra, I think those pictures you got were of Whit. And I think she's the angel who sent you that cash."

She gasped, her lips popping like a hooked fish. "Where in the world did she get her hands on that kind of money, Rook?"

"I don't know. I'm working on it. Give me another few days. I'll report back to you and Leola."

"But what can I tell her now?"

"Tell her I've seen her child. Tell her she's okay. I won't promise she's completely safe yet. And of course, I can't promise to bring her back."

"You have to try. You've *got* to." The urgency pulled Sondra from her seat.

"That choice is up to her. But she's alive and healthy and has people looking out for her."

"You know more than you're saying, right?"

I nodded to keep her in my camp. "Sondra, I get it. These are skimpy crumbs. But I hope Leola can take a little comfort from what I've shared."

As Brina and I rose to go, Sondra took my hand, squeezing it hard. "I'll tell Leola. I know you'll keep pushing for more. And you'll let us know when you find out anything. Anything at all."

"I will."

"And if you see him, let Whit know he's loved here." Sondra's dark eyes shimmered under their burden of tears.

"I'll tell him." I tried to follow Sondra's lead, but the pronoun hitched on my tongue.

"Tell him his mother, me, Keisha, all of us. We're worried sick about him and we love him. As he is. Whenever he's ready to come back, we're ready to have him. As he is." She squeezed my fingers, forcing her sincerity into my knuckles until they stung.

"I'll let her–Whit – know. You have my word." I tried "him," but the three letters skipped and twisted until they slid down my throat unspoken.

———————————

As we left the old church, I dragged to Brina's car. This was a lot to take in, and I wasn't sure I could do it with Brina watching. She had already cranked up the air conditioning by the time I buckled the seat belt. "Like Sondra said, your eyes say you got ideas charging through your head. You want to share?"

"Don't know if I can." I shifted as the cushion pumped heat under my thighs.

Brina's interrogator voice softened. "It's a lot to take in. I didn't get a good look at the kid. In the park we were too far away for me to see. But you followed for all those blocks. Did you know he was trans?"

"No. Didn't cross my mind. He was just a kid in trouble. That's what I saw."

"That's still true."

"Yes, but I don't know what to think about it."

"Does it make a difference to your investigation?"

"No. It shouldn't."

"But it does?"

"Yes. It does."

"Can you say why?"

"No. I don't know, Brina. I'm sorting it out." I released a long draft of air as she steered around a taxi stopped for a grocery-juggling shopper. "I'll do it. Just takes some time."

We rode in silence to the office. We stayed quiet for the rest of the afternoon, Brina pecking at her computer in the reception area, me slumped at my desk.

Whitney, Whit, Whip. The names changed; the kid stuck to his truth. Looming over it all was the pile of money, unclaimed and dangerous.

CHAPTER
NINE

Early evenings at Zarita's bar were my sometime ritual.

I spent an hour across the street from our office nursing a bourbon when work was slack. Or when a client had burned through my reserve of patience. Or the sun scorched the breeze and singed holes in the sticky asphalt. Or the neighborhood shimmered in a transparent gel under its burden of heat.

Or when I just needed a break. Then I dropped into the bar for a breather. I didn't go to Zarita's every day, that would be an addiction, not a hobby. I hadn't made friends with the regulars who glued their haunches to the wooden stools and screwed their elbows into the brass countertop of the central bar every night. Too much familiarity and I'd pass for a drunk. But I knew the name of the bartender, Jerome Stewart, because he'd given me a few good tips, steered me clear of blunders or pointed me toward puzzle pieces I'd missed in the past. He'd also hired me for a few cases involving his own wayward son, Pence. My usual spot in Zarita's was in the last booth in the back, past the swinging doors that led to the bathrooms. That booth enjoyed the best access to the shaky air conditioner hanging high on the wall.

So, that's where I headed when five-thirty made quitting the office acceptable. As Brina watched me slink toward the outer door, tears danced along her lower lids, trapping the light from the dying sun into little jewels among her lashes. She wanted me to talk; I wanted her to share. I wasn't ready. Might never be ready. She seemed reluctant too. I stopped at her desk, then leaned across it to tap her chin with my index finger, lifting her face until the tears receded. Nothing to say, I stayed silent and she did too.

Bourbon clung like sludge to the ice in my glass for the first hour. The second drink slipped down faster, which made the third a bewitching possibility. I hadn't signaled Jerome to bring the next round. But it arrived anyway, in the fat right hand of my pal Archie Lin. In his left, Archie gripped two long-necked bottles of Michelob, a glass clinging in desperation to his pinky finger. He must have been a champion waiter in his prime.

"Bartender said you ordered this." Archie pushed the short glass of brown liquor toward me without ceremony.

"I didn't. But thanks anyway, Detective."

Archie squeezed his thick frame onto the bench opposite and took a heavy pull from the first bottle. Then he poured the rest of the beer into the glass, as if he'd remembered his manners all of a sudden. He was still wearing the suit from his official day: exhaust-fume gray with a faint yellow chalk stripe, powder blue shirt open at the collar. He'd lost the tie somewhere, which was good. Thinking of his neck throttled by stray cloth caused sweat to trickle down my back. I could count on one finger the times Archie had joined me for a drink in Zarita's. He preferred more upscale watering holes for our get-togethers. On a city salary, he could afford the high-priced joints, so I let him host me.

It was easy to guess how he'd arrived at Zarita's. "Brina steer you this way?"

"She might have leaked something on your whereabouts when she picked up Pinky."

The two girlfriends had a standing date for the fourth Thursday of each month. It was that time of the month again. Hah. Brina was probably scarfing tiny appetizers in some elegant restaurant with Pinky, spilling her pregnancy story. And roasting me in the telling: my flinty loner habits, my closed mouth moodiness. I was sure she had plenty to say about my deficits as father material too. My low pay, low ambition, and herd of low friends in the gutters, brothels, and hobo camps of Harlem disqualified me for parenthood, she'd say. I was a scrub with a sad sack's frayed portfolio. Growing up without a father myself, how could I have the first clue about being a father now? For sure, Brina was downing virgin Bloody Marys and giving her friend an earful of complaints about me.

With Pinky occupied, Archie lacked a wife for the evening and searched for me as a sorry substitute. "How many ahead of me are you, pal?"

I shrugged. "Not enough." Archie couldn't jerk me from my brooding with such a simple maneuver. I took another sip, which dribbled into a slurp.

Archie frowned at my rude noises. "Slow your roll, amigo." He fingered the pile of napkins next to the salt shaker, looking for a menu. "Doesn't this dive make sandwiches or something?"

We ordered four toasted cheese sandwiches. Toasted cheese was the only dish Zarita's offered, but the plain, sticky goodness suited the bar's honesty. And someone in the kitchen was a skillet-wielding Picasso: that cheddar melting into rye was genius on a plate. After the food arrived, Archie unpacked his current cases. And asked about mine. The overlap brought us to the drive-by murder of Zaire Martin. I sketched my conversations at the homeless camp and my discovery of the hidden identity of Z's friend, Whip Covington.

"Did you know the kid was trans?" Archie's question doubled down on Brina's from earlier in the day.

"No. I didn't see it. Just a kid in trouble. That's what I saw."

"Doesn't make any difference, does it? This Whip kid's got intel, you need to find him. Or her. Whatever."

"Right."

"But there's more." No questioning rise at the end of his sentence, but the demand was clear. "It means something to you, doesn't it? This boy-girl thing."

I nodded and rotated the glass. "What am I supposed to call Whip, when I find her?"

" 'Hey you!' works pretty good on my block. Try that."

"Not what I mean, Archie."

"Then go with the usual: 'punk.'"

I stepped into the game. "Or 'jerk.'"

"Yeah, sure. But if you want fancy, use 'asshole.' Accurate one hundred percent of the time. Trust me."

"*Pendéjo.*"

"Sure, that's okay in your Spanish precincts. But you want maximum impact, you flash the black card and drop the N-bomb. Black dude privilege works every time."

"Think that'll get the kid's attention?"

"Guaranteed. Of course, it might also get you a split lip. How big did you say this chick was anyway?"

"She wants to be called 'he.'"

"So, try it. Use 'he.'"

"She's a *girl*, Arch."

"So? You're a dick. With a dick."

"Like you."

"Yeah, like me." Half smile around the mouth of the beer bottle. "What do you care what sticky parts are between whose legs anyway? That don't matter to this case, do it?"

"No." I puffed a short breath over my glass. "But you don't let go of something like that. Not easily. Not ever."

Archie drilled his eyes into mine. "You mean: *you* don't."

"No. I don't. I can't." The ice shifted under its bourbon veil and I studied it hard.

"And you see some kind of perversion here? A religion thing? You think Whip's wrong for being trans?"

"No. Not wrong." That certainty drifted on the chilled air chugging from the machine above our heads. "But I still have to work on what I think."

Archie Lin was a good friend. He knew when to interrupt, when to challenge, when to correct. And when to shut the hell up.

He stayed quiet as I finished. "Here's what I do know: Whip's in trouble. Big money trouble. The killing kind of trouble. I have a case and he's my client." *Maybe this pronoun thing might get easier, if I practiced. A lot.* "I know one fact, Archie. I've got work to do. And Whip's my job. I won't back off. Simple as that."

Archie grunted the echo, "Simple as that," and flattened his hand over the damp table. "Don't go this alone, Rook. If this case is police business, you come to us when you got something we should know."

"Yeah, sure, Arch."

Simple. Not a chance. But as we chewed, the crumbs dropped, and our talk shifted. Dead guys we'd met. Live women we'd known. A dog or two in both columns. Archie's two Michelobs didn't equal my three bourbons. His cheeks flamed orange, but my ankles wobbled like licorice stalks. By the end of the evening, Archie won the sober derby. Grand prize was the privilege of driving me home.

As I tipped to the door of my building, I fingered the squirmy mass of rubber bands in my pocket. I pulled out one red elastic and examined its ragged ends. I might be blitzed, but I was right: the money gifted to Friends In Deed had been wrapped with the same rubber bands I'd found in the backpack in Odette's stash. Now my job was to trim and stretch, jolt and snap these pieces until they fit the puzzle. And save Whip. *Whoever. However.*

CHAPTER
TEN

Another day and still no word from Whip.

Like a salt-bloated slug, I clung to my desk, the office air thickening with dread each time the phone rang. I unraveled the ball of red rubber bands and laid them in formations on my desk. First end-to-end along the perimeter. Then as a wobbly elastic moat around my cell phone. No matter how I arranged them, the rubber bands refused to reveal their purpose.

Norment was absent on assignment, and by the end of the afternoon, my restless silence defeated Brina's patience. She left to meet her hairdresser friend Lourene for a drink, no invitation extended to me. My solemn scowl would harsh their vibe for sure. So, I decided to enjoy happy hour alone in my office. I drafted the Jim Beam bottle in the bottom drawer of my desk to the cause. The glass was short, but filling it to the brim made a healthy portion. I downed that and then another swig, smaller but just as mighty. The bourbon burned, but didn't relieve my conscience. Commitment to Sondra Crane and Friends In Deed pressed on me, the weight clammy and wet like a tarp. With each hour, the danger to Whip expanded. He might not realize it, but I did. Rather than finish my boozy dinner with a third round, I hit the street, walking off the ugly buzz with a goal in mind.

I paid another visit to Whip's only known address: the homeless camp presided over by Eddie, the prince of paupers. The kid might be there, consulting with his mentor in rags. I could corner him and plot a way out of the danger. Or at least ease my worries for another night.

Dusk covered my arrival at the entrance of the Palace. Odette filled the door frame, dazzling in layers of aqua and lime-green mesh. She looked like meringue frosting on stilts. The old woman recognized me; at least, I think the jig of her brows meant that. But if she recalled our previous encounter on the street corner, she didn't let on.

"Hey, you. With the crazy gorgeous eyes. I know you." Without missing a beat, this last phrase led Odette into a burst of fairy-tale waltz. Was she the Sleeping Beauty in this song? Or was I?

She twirled, then dropped her eyes, waiting for applause. Like that dream, her voice had been beautiful once. But now, age, rough hooch, drugs, and curbside living had scratched the glitter. She squeaked and strained in the high notes and ran out of breath before the end of the longer passages. But when I clapped, she ducked into a deep curtsey, a true performer delighted to please a new audience. Our encounter on the street and my inspection of her shopping cart didn't matter. Only the applause.

"Odette, I've come to see Eddie. Is he in?" Booze slowed my words to fake patience.

"Of course, Eddie's in. Like always. Where else would he be? Come on up and rest your fine bones a spell." I held the door for her, and Odette brushed past me and up the stairs, her gauzy skirts swishing dust from each step as she moved.

Eddie sat on his mattress-throne, legs stiff in front of him as before. The gold knit cap had disappeared; his gray hair bristled in a wiry halo around his head. He'd unbuttoned his purple wool coat in concession to the stifling heat. As Odette and I approached, Eddie stared at a far corner of the vast warehouse, his eyes darting as if focused on a movie screen only he could view.

"Hey, Odette, you're back." After this thin greeting and a nod at me, he resumed his vigil.

Ever the dutiful hostess, Odette waved me toward a trampled corner of their mattress. "Pull up a chair, doll. Eddie'll come around after a while." Her eyes were tight and her smile toothless, like a sitcom housewife waiting for hubby to return home.

I sat, plucking my shirt from my chest to create a breeze. I wanted to ask him about Whip and the other boys of the green backpack brigade. But the moment demanded silence, so I waited. Against expectation, Odette stifled herself too.

After five minutes Eddie spoke, casting his reedy tenor toward the old rafters. "Bad things went down here today. Real bad things."

He was her man; it was Odette's place to respond. But she blinked and said nothing, so I tried. "What happened, Eddie?"

"Odette told me I shouldn't ever tell sad stories. Not to her, not to anyone."

"But, Eddie, you know you can talk with me." I was a member of his court now. Counsellor or jester, maybe both. "I won't tell anyone. Not unless you say I can."

The old man pursed his lips, then nodded, the movement of his head rocking his whole body. He stared toward the far end of the warehouse, bleary eyes tracking a scene disconnected from the pantomime of the people clustered in small groups there.

"I saw that girl Kendya again today. Odette remembers her. Kendya. Tall, polite enough, pretty brown skin, but cross-eyed. She used to come around most mornings, searching for breakfast and such. I gave her what I could spare. A few others did too."

Eddie dropped into his cinema, fingers rubbing the furrows at the side of his mouth. I hesitated to rouse him. But I wanted to know the story. Imitating his gestures, I touched my lips and looked toward the shimmering sky, waiting. Then I prompted again. "What was she doing, Eddie? You can tell me. It won't hurt her."

"No, Kendya can't be hurt no more. You're right about that, Rook." He sighed and stroked the skin of his poreless, dark face. "That sick girl had a devil habit eating her alive. And she was sucking dick for dollars to buy the coke she needed. Other people do it; she wasn't special, that's for sure. But it was a real shame all the same."

Odette gasped, a wet mournful sound lapping at my ears. Eddie's story hit close to home. I closed my eyes. I'd walked that block, tripped over cracks in that pavement. I didn't want this to be anybody's story. But I needed to hear how it ended. "What happened to her, Eddie?"

"Kendya died, or got killed, or just stopped living. I don't know which. This morning when I saw her, she was dead, lying stiff over in that corner down there." Eddie swept his gnarled hand toward the far end of the building.

"Everybody was gathered around in a clump, so I went to see what the racket was. That girl was lying on her back, her eyes and mouth open, her hands clutched in front of her like she was trying to climb a wall. People were pulling at her clothing, tearing at her coat, her shoes, her dress, her scarf."

Eddie stopped to rub a finger into the puffy flesh above his right eye. "It was horrible, Rook. I never saw nothing like it. They tore everything off her, looking for money or drugs. Even her underwear. They flung her jacket off to one side after they turned the pockets inside out and found a few bills. I snatched the jacket. I felt a lump under the lining next to the sleeve. It was a safety pin with something fastened inside. I turned my back so they couldn't see what I was doing, and I tore the lining. It was a little gold ring with a purple stone she had pinned inside the jacket."

The old man sobbed once, a dry hack that rattled his chest. "Amethyst it was. Prettiest purple you ever want to see. I took that ring, Rook. I took it; it was wrong. God forgive me, I took it and kept it for myself."

Tears like wet seeds rustled under the notch at my throat, choking me. Tears for Kendya. For Odette and Eddie. For myself. "What happened to the body, Eddie?"

"They stuffed her into an oil drum and burned her like trash, that's what happened."

"And the ring?"

"I saved it for Odette. I couldn't keep it. But I couldn't throw it away neither. Amethyst is February's birth stone. Odette's born in February. So, I'm giving it to you, girl." He turned and presented the ring on the crooked tip of his little finger. "You can wear it on that chain around your neck."

Odette took it without a smile, rolled it in her palm for a few seconds and then fished a long silver chain from the bodice of her dress. With delicate movements, she unfastened the necklace and ran the links through the gold ring. Then she draped the chain over her head again and tucked the gift down her bosom.

Silence consumed us. For several minutes, the couple's thoughts ran along parallel paths, then converged in a simultaneous burst.

Odette in soprano: "Don't let me die like that, Eddie. Nobody to mourn me, nobody to name me."

Eddie in tenor: "Promise me you won't let that happen to me either."

"It won't. You have my word, baby."

More silence, this time calmer. I coughed to change the subject, to drag us from Eddie's miserable story. Maybe the new topic wouldn't be upbeat, but I tossed it anyway. "Eddie, have you heard from that kid, Whip?"

"No. You?" The old man's focus sharpened, like a knife striking stone. His brows flew, brightness jumping from his yellowed eyes. Relieved, like me, to talk about something other than the cold isolation of death.

"Not a peep. I was wondering if you had a chance to give him my card like I asked you the other day."

"Yeah, I gave it to him the next night. Don't know what he did with it. You better give me another one, just for safe keeping."

I handed him a fresh Ross Agency card. Eddie admired it as he'd done the first time: caressing the address and then the embossed letters of my name. Then he traced along the circle of the red-outlined pupil in the center of the agency's staring eye logo. After a minute, he stuffed the card into his hair and patted down the coils for added security. "I'll make sure Whip gets this. Count on it, Rook."

As Eddie filed my card, Odette tugged on the silver chain around her neck, drawing the ring from its hiding place. She studied the pale purple stone like a cherished family heirloom she hadn't seen in decades. Then she turned a thin smile on me. "Thank you for letting me wear it, Rook. I took good care of it for you, see?"

Odette giggled, a girl blushing before a suitor, and dropped her eyes. Then she bowed from the waist. The woman's gentle confusion enveloped me in sorrow. I needed to escape before I suffocated.

"After a while…See you 'round… Check you later." The empty phrases released me. I crossed the broad wooden floor in a few strides.

When I reached the staircase, I looked back. Eddie had his arm around Odette's shoulders. They were crying, foreheads pressed together for solace. But a quick brush of pastel taffeta across both faces erased their tears and they smiled at each other again. Then Odette thought of a new tune. A song that promised love, if only for a moment, floating on faith in forever.

I plunged through the door, leaped steps on my way down. I forgot to rub the guardian goddess at the gateway as I left.

CHAPTER
ELEVEN

The melancholy encounter with my hobo informants sobered me. Rather than drift home for a lonely meeting with the microwave, I headed toward a cup of coffee at Lonnie's Diner.

My favorite waitress, Raye, doled out generous helpings of neighborhood gossip along with her high-test brew. She was the flirty aunt I'd never had, the forever cool embodiment of comfort food and down-home common sense. Raye refused to indulge my complaints, guilt, or occasional paranoia. She was a fierce rainbow coalition of one, a pride parade without the pom-poms and marching band. "I'm old-style, baby. I might be gay," she told me. "But my talk is straight. Don't come 'round here if you want sugar, Sugar." A sip of Raye's tartness would perk up the groggy evening.

Lonnie's was four blocks from the Palace. As I crossed the first intersection, movement flickered in the laundromat window to my right. The yellow interior shone in harsh contrast to the shadows of the surrounding street. Beyond the glass, two women in flowered shorts and tight t-shirts worked the washing machines. A baby in a sagging diaper crawled between little heaps of powder detergent on the linoleum.

In the foreground, a dark silhouette hovered, then darted as I passed. Something about the shape of the head and the glide of the walk seemed familiar, so I cut my pace. The figure slowed. I sped double-time for the next block and my tail scooted to stay in range. Usually, I tracked the quarry, prey didn't stalk me. But being followed was flattering. If someone cared enough to pursue me, I was intrigued.

The shadow followed me across another intersection, clinging to the dark stains on the sidewalks between the pools of lamplight. I walked fast, then cruised, then revved the pace again. I didn't try to lose my tail by slipping beside a roving pedestrian. I wanted to test the tracking skills of my follower, but I didn't want to lose him.

After ten minutes of this chase, I rolled into Lonnie's Diner at a good clip and skidded across the blue-and-white tile floor to my special booth. As I settled on the bench facing the front of the room, Whip pushed through the door.

She dropped into a seat at a rickety table near the entrance. Points of red flecked her brown cheeks and she panted to catch a breath. For an old man, I'd given her a pretty good run. A damp triangle darkened the collar of her t-shirt, turning its dusky red into maroon where cloth touched skin. Sagging jeans stopped at her calves above white high-top sneakers with the classic Nike swoop. The black hair was spikey and dull with grime. This was the closest I'd gotten, my first chance for a detailed survey. From across the room, the kid looked like a butched-up girl. But I tried the guy pronouns in my head anyway. *He, not she. Him, not her.* Practice makes perfect.

Whip pressed his back to the wall, stowing a deflated green backpack under his chair. Slouching, legs wide in a macho spread, he glanced at me, dark eyes blazing under strong brows. He plunked a phone onto the table top, then poked its face. He stuck a cord into the phone then plugged his ears with tiny buds. A zoned-out satisfaction drifted across his eyes, the smug look of a purring cat as it ignores you. The kid hoisted a laminated menu in front of his face. When Raye came for his order, he waved her off. Then he called her back with a whispered request.

Three minutes later Raye bounced to my booth with a plated slab of apple pie. *A la mode.*

"Hey, Fancy Face. Looks like you got yourself a little fan club over there." She rolled her eyes in the direction of Whip.

"I didn't order this." Irritation made me snap. Annoyance bent my voice into a whine, and I glared. "Take it back."

Raye didn't cower. She ran a hand under the flip of tangerine curls at the nape of her neck. A straight middle finger, nail lacquered in neon purple polish, pointed in my direction. To make sure I got that message, she added a crisp slice of advice: "Whatever's eating your craw, Rook, you best leave it outside. Just because you got pretty eyes don't mean you get away with smart mouthing me, ya know. I'm immune to them beauties, got the vaccine shots and all." She patted her ass to complete the picture.

If the eyes wouldn't work, I tried another tactic. I tipped my head and smirked. "Aww, Raye, I'm not looking to aggravate you. You know that. Just got a few things on my mind. And one of them's that boy over there." I raised my chin in Whip's direction. He was still hidden behind the plastic menu.

"*Boy*? Oh, is that right? Well, okay, if you say so. Looks like a girl wasting time passing for a boy. But you're the big fancy detective. I'm just a little old lesbian grubbing for tips." Raye co-owned the diner with her longtime partner Lonnie, so the modest assessment of her status was pure fakery.

Tilting her gelled head toward Whip, she explained: "Kid said you looked like you needed pie, so I recommended the apple. It's today's special. Last slice in the pan. Take it or leave it, Rook. Kid's paying."

I didn't want to be in Whip's debt, even a little bit. I pushed the plate toward the edge of the table.

But a quick shadow intervened. "We'll take it, Raye. Thanks." Glossy with cheer, Brina slipped into the high-backed booth opposite me and grabbed the plate before Raye could remove it. She skipped the greeting and went straight for the fork, unwrapping it from the paper napkin and brandishing it over the pie with intent. "I'm hungry, if you're not."

It had only been a few hours since she quit the office for her drinks date. But even so, seeing her now, Brina looked good to me, rested and fresh, golden cheeks shiny from the sun, brown eyes bright with mischief and love. I took a deep breath and lowered my lids. Could it be true? After such a brief absence, did I miss her already? Keeping this hard-boiled pose going was tougher than it seemed in the movies.

The Brina effect was like stepping onto the fire escape in a fresh spring shower. Cool, alert, all senses firing at once–colors sharp, sounds crisp, the air flicked at the hair on my arms and smells dazzled with new vigor. The pie smelled good: tart and sweet with the spices of vanilla and cinnamon curling into the buttery scent of the crust. Brina smelled good too, her amber and bright green scent tugging on my heart.

"How did you know where to find me?" The simpleton line was weak, but my safest approach.

She smiled at me. "After Lourene and I split, I made an educated guess where you were headed. So, I popped into Lonnie's."

No way that was true. Brina had checked first in Zarita's Bar before landing at the diner. But I loved her casual lie and her knowledge of me. She got my moods and forgave them. In advance. I picked up a teaspoon and scraped a flake off the buttery crust. Brina could have the ice cream, but the apple pie was too inviting to pass. Sharing the task, we dived into the dessert like nomads at an oasis well. The pie disappeared in two minutes.

Brina slid her phone next to the empty plate and punched in a number. "I told Daddy I'd call him when I found you. He said he had something he wanted to share with us."

She put the phone on speaker and pushed it toward me. I didn't think the kid could hear me from his seat across the room, but I lowered my voice all the same. "Whip's over there. Against the wall near the door."

Either to mock me or because he really didn't care, the boy let his eyes drift toward the quilted aluminum on the restaurant ceiling. Then bopped his head to the secret beats of his jam. Instead of turning to look at Whip, Brina squinted, then eye rolled in quick succession. All while fiddling with the speaker button on her phone. Real silent movie talent.

As Brina tapped at the cell phone and the kid grooved in the corner, I held my breath. When the old private eye picked up, I launched the conversation. "Norment, what've you got? Make it good."

CHAPTER
TWELVE

Norment Ross skipped greetings, preamble, or set up—got right to the point, a departure from his regular all-around-the-barn country style. Norment's message was more important, or more dire, than usual.

"I had lunch today with Imelda, this lady friend of mine who works in the U.S. Attorney's office in Brooklyn. We go back a ways, and I like to keep connections with her. Treading light, you know. I never like to cut off anybody just because we went through a rough patch a few years ago."

"And what did she have to say, Daddy?" Brina was the one to push this forward, so I stayed quiet.

But I couldn't help twitching a corner of my mouth. Norment's network of female friends stretched across the five boroughs. The old man had a special relationship with our landlady, the restaurant owner Mei Young. Their close ties went back decades. Maybe that agreement allowed Norment room to pursue old flames like Imelda, if the results were strictly professional. I valued my neck and my job too much to risk asking. Listening in silence to Norment's story was my best option.

"Imelda made me promise to hold this close. But soon as she told me, I knew it could fit in with things you all are working on, so I'm spilling it to you anyway."

The boss gathered his breath for a long sentence with a payload of heavy words.

"She told me federal prosecutors are putting together a case about some kind of cybercrime attack against major international financial institutions. You know, banks and credit unions and such like. According to Imelda, the operation they're investigating involves laundering millions of dollars stolen from banks across the city in a matter of hours."

"Sounds sexy, Norment. Your gal Imelda sure knows how to crank a good story, doesn't she?" I chuckled and leaned back on the bench.

But Norment didn't adopt the light tone; he delivered the story in a slow pace, his baritone somber and deliberate. *"Rook, this one's as serious as a heart attack. No time for joshing here."* This was Norment at his frostiest. But since he was on the other end of the line, I kept smiling. He continued: *"Imelda told me the feds are looking at a fancy load of money laundering. I'm talking a scheme which passes the stolen money through purchases of luxury items like Rolex watches and expensive cars, condos, even yachts."*

The pause after this declaration would have re-frozen the ice cream if there was any left on the plate. I stared at Brina as her father poured out his fantastic story. *"We're not talking Monopoly money here. Over three hundred ATM machines in New York City were hit in a ten-hour span on four separate occasions since last May. Each time the haul from these withdrawals added up to at least a half million dollars."*

Norment said nothing more, as if the scope of the operation was so enormous it left even a seasoned street runner like him in awe. Brina lowered her mouth to the phone. Astonishment wreathed her face and her words squeaked with tension. "Daddy, do you think this has something to do with shooting Zaire in the park? How does our kid come into something gigantic like this kind of operation?"

"I'm not sure, baby girl. So far, the feds don't seem to know too much about how the operation is organized. They have a pretty clear idea of the middle layer of this operation. They got indictments—still sealed–against the people they believe are responsible for laundering the money. But the prosecutors still don't know who the front-line soldiers are. And they're stumped on who could be the mastermind at the top of the whole shebang."

"You think Whip --" Brina breathed the name on a whisper. "-- and his crew might be the ones carrying out the heists?"

I checked, but the head-bobbing boy across the room didn't look our way. Scorn crisped my voice. "Norment, these kids aren't even out of high school. How do you figure Whip and his friends pull off a complicated financial racket like that?"

"Like I said, Rook, I don't know. And neither do the federal boys. Imelda said they're slam up against a brick wall a hundred miles high on this one. But I do know this for sure: the mind directing this operation has a mighty powerful grasp. A person like that has to have a knack for pulling together millions of little details. Moving around computers, people, money, fancy goods in a dance that turns in the blink of an eye. And, on top of that, I figure whoever it is has a real sick kind of artistry. This is somebody who thinks big picture, and has the balls to bring his imagination to life."

Norment paused, as if struck dumb by the specter he had raised with these images. *"So maybe, if you keep that kid Whip in your sights, you might get a chance to ask him yourself about the spider at the center of this whole web."*

I looked across the aisle. Whip was thrusting his chin and cranking his neck in time to the music's hidden thump.

A few words more and Norment signed off, promising to check with us if he learned additional details. Imelda had asked him to dinner Saturday night, so if he played his cards right, he might get lucky in more ways than one before the weekend was over.

As Brina returned the phone to her pocket, I glanced toward the restaurant door. A lanky man with a bush of thick black coils and a cocky stride advanced on Whip's table at a rapid pace. His wispy beard suggested he was just out of his teens, his dark dull skin and ashy hands meant he spent lots of time outdoors. Baggy black jeans and a black t-shirt were set off by a blazing red bandanna knotted around his tattooed neck. He carried a heavy backpack identical to the green one at Whip's feet.

This was Link, the skinny geranium wrangler we'd spotted on Mrs. Lowery's front porch the previous week. The Link who'd displayed his knife skills on my shirt and ear at the Palace.

The newcomer stood over Whip without a smile, one intense stare matched by the other. When he bent, my hand spasmed around the spoon. Whip slanted his smooth cheek to the man, then raised his palm for a high five. The ease, even joy of the gesture hit me so hard I dropped the spoon. The two bumped fists, then Link draped himself over the chair opposite Whip.

"Calm down, Papa Bear, that's no murder attempt." Brina flattened her hands on the table, reaching toward me as the spoon clattered on the floor. Her tone was light, teasing me out of my alarm. "Maybe a love match." Brina crinkled her eyes until they disappeared. "I think they're cute."

I huffed, agreeing in spite of myself.

"You're supposed to protect Whip from assassins, Rook, not sexy friends. So, stand down, soldier."

Whip and Link spent only a few moments in animated conversation before placing their order with Raye.

Smiles wreathed both faces, Whip's brilliant and so open with optimism a superstitious chill crept along my spine as I watched them. Link's teeth were stained by years of smoking. Whip's were white but small, framed like a child's in bright pink gums. Whip looked happy and oblivious. That dangerous combination sent dread crackling across my nervous system. But I kept my thoughts to myself as I listened to Brina sketch out the resolution of a case she'd wrestled with the day before.

"I handed him over to Archie Lin with only a split lip and a gunshot wound to the calf. That joker was lucky to get off so easy. He deserved a plug between the eyes." Brina tilted her head to one side, waiting to draw a laugh from me.

I grunted but remained silent, still watching the pair across the room. When the skinny man sprang to his feet, I started out of my trance. Link looked straight at me, a sneer twisting his mouth. He winked and tugged at his left ear, then raised an eyebrow. Without thinking, I touched the thread he'd sliced behind my earlobe; pain still nipped at the scab. Gripping a backpack, Link tapped Whip on the shoulder and swept out the door.

Brina was fast to notice the bug. "Did you see that? Ebony Romeo's backpack was heavy when he walked in here. But flat and empty when he left."

I nodded and sucked my teeth in recognition. "They switched. It was a hand-off."

Whip edged from behind his table, leaving two bills next to his empty shake glass. He slung the heavy backpack over his right shoulder as he left the restaurant, heading in the opposite direction to the one taken by his friend. Brina and I followed at a close distance. We shrank into the shadowed entrance of a nail salon when Whip stopped at a corner after walking for two blocks.

When the light turned green, he didn't cross the intersection, but looked with round eyes in all four directions. He was waiting for someone.

"The car!" I pointed at a black sedan with smoke-tinted windows, idling in a bus stop at the curb. "Get rid of the driver. I'll take the kid."

Brina stepped around the car, shoulders strong, chin jutting forward. She flipped the hem of her shirt to reveal the gun holstered on her belt. The driver bolted from the vehicle. His lips flapped, saliva flew, and he split the curbside crowd, leaving the key in the ignition.

I glanced again at Whip. A thick man grabbed his shoulder and then his elbow. The man, no taller than Whip, wrapped an arm across the boy's chest and dragged him toward the getaway car. The brute's biceps strained below the short sleeves of his green polo shirt. His bulging neck rooted like a tree in the collar's *V*. Pressed two-twenty on a good day, maybe two-forty. Too bad pumping iron didn't give him eyes in the rear of his shaved head.

With his back turned, the thug didn't see me step into his path. When he drew alongside the sedan, he shouted an order. His head rotated in a neat circle, the orbit intersecting with my fist. The first jab crunched like a walnut in a vise: the crack meaty and good. Bone hit bone; sinew bent to force. He yelped; the high-pitched scream caused pedestrians to crane their necks. Whip squirmed, freeing an arm. With a short thrust, he drove his elbow into the goon's midsection. Tough kid. The man bowed, wind spewing from clenched teeth. My next blow, a power slug to the temple, dropped him. Knees thudded, torso caved, and pink jumped from under the peeled hide of both elbows.

I bent over his heaving body to memorize the man's features. He was dark, a blueish undertone to the skin, five-seven or eight, maybe forty years old. Brawny and top-heavy, muscles stacked on his shoulders like center cut sirloin slabs. But thirty seconds was too long to waste studying this goon; he might have pals nearby.

I clamped a hand around Whip's arm and swung him toward the car door. "We need to get somewhere safe. Now. Move."

I pushed the kid into the back seat and fell on top of him. Brina slipped behind the wheel. She gunned the engine, pounding the pedal without a backward glance. She peeled from the bus stop before I slammed the door shut. Curses in Farsi, English, Spanish, and Russian escorted us into the clogged lane. Brina flipped a one finger salute to the other drivers as we passed. They were lucky she didn't kiss some random bumpers with this stolen car. Or empty her gun into their tires.

Next to me, Whip exhaled. The long gust blew surly, mournful, and shocked before it shuddered to a halt. I flexed my fingers, testing the scrapes on my knuckles. One split, one scratch, one gouge. Soap-and-water level damage. Grand theft auto, misdemeanor assault, and felony kidnapping. Our crime spree was a small price to pay for answers from the elusive kid at the center of this case.

CHAPTER
THIRTEEN

Chaos drove the evening traffic. Gathering gloom and the darting of brazen pedestrians complicated the uptown congestion. Brina's brow furrowed in concentration as she maneuvered the unfamiliar car, a heavy foot on the pedal. I hadn't suggested where to go. I didn't have any ideas. In the crisis, I didn't care where we went. My only need was to be far from the men trying to harm Whip. Brina's mouth set in a firm line. She didn't ask questions or give any clue where we were headed. With no definite destination in mind, I let her lead.

As we careened through the streets, the kid pressed into a corner of the bench, clutching the thick backpack against his stomach, staring through the darkened windows at the passing scene. He said nothing. This was my first chance to examine him. From a distance, I'd thought he was sixteen. But now noting the fine hands and soft lips, fourteen fit better. The long chin and lowered brow came from his mother, Leola Covington.

From a distance, I'd been wrong about other things too. Up close, Whip looked female. Round cheeks, smooth jaws padded with baby fat. Sparse eyebrows and a gentle slope to the throat. A girl's face. The wrinkled red t-shirt disguised the figure underneath. But the faded animé cartoon character on it said she treasured childhood memories. Whip's black hair sprung at uneven angles above her high forehead; she couldn't afford the regular barbershop visits required to keep a neat cut. Her skin was soft, untouched by a razor despite hopes for adult male status.

After fifteen minutes of erratic lane changes, jarring stops, and sudden jags, the neighborhood turned familiar. We arrived at my apartment six minutes later. Brina pulled into the loading zone at the building's entrance. The street was quiet; we were in the clear.

"Nobody followed us." I sounded more confident than I felt.

"Yeah, maybe. But don't hang around the curb. In case you're wrong." Miss Bonnie Parker took her getaway driver role to heart. "I'll ditch the car. See you as soon as I can."

Whip and I hustled through the lobby for the elevator to my apartment.

———————

"You some kind of a ninja spy? This your idea of a safe house?"

Whip's voice shot through the room as I stepped aside to let her enter. Simple pronouns butted each other as I looked at the kid. Talking out loud was easier– "you" worked for most sentences. But in my head, "her" shuffled beside "him" and "she" pushed aside "he."

Confusion caused the stutter. "No—no, I didn't say that, exactly."

"Exactly? Or at all?"

"No, not a spy." I looked around, seeing the cramped space through the kid's critical eyes.

The queen-size bed was neat, if sway-backed. The powder blue coverlet looked okay; Brina said the blue did something for my eyes, so despite the worn patches I hadn't replaced it. I stowed my jeans, trousers, and shirts in the closet. But a wrinkled suit jacket slouched on the room's lone armchair. And a nest of castoff socks tangled under the table. The place looked empty, neglected. How could I protect somebody else if I didn't attend to my own meager possessions? Right off the bat, I'd failed this kid in my care. How could I pretend to have the skills necessary for taking care of a child of my own? I shoved my hands into my pockets and looked at the carpet. Herb, my yellow cat, wound his big body around my ankles, purring as loud as a Saturday morning garbage truck. At least Herb approved. I waited for a snarky jab from the kid.

But then Whip spoke again, her bright chirp a welcome intrusion in the silence: "Oh man, this is just what I need, cold water!"

He ran to the kitchen sink, tossing his backpack on the bed. He cranked the faucet and plunged his hands into the basin four times. Then he rubbed the soap bar until it gave a thick lather and he cleaned his face. When he'd toweled off, he turned on the water again, cupping his hands to take several deep drinks.

Satisfied, he looked over his shoulder at me. "This looks pretty safe." His deep-set eyes swept from one side of the room to the other, then fixed on me. "Thanks for your help."

Pure gratitude flooded through me in that moment. I wanted to hug him for this simple declaration. Instead of getting mushy, I kept my balance by throwing a question I'd held for some time: "You weren't ever scared of me, were you?"

"No, why would I be?" Whip laughed then, his wide mouth stretching in merriment. His voice was childish, light, and musical. "I clocked you when you first came to the Palace that night. After the shooting. You were staring at me. Sorta creepy, but in a funny way; weirdo but not nasty."

Whip's attention lighted on Herb and he stooped low, clucking to lure the cat. Herb trotted to him without hesitation, the ultimate endorsement of a finicky judge.

"And then you kept following me. But you never attacked, so I figured you weren't bad. I thought maybe you were some kind of perv. But the bashful kind, not a sicko molester. Or maybe just super curious."

I kicked off my sneakers as he continued the assessment of me. He took in my wrinkled white shirt, the slick of sweat at my throat, the day's grime around my collar, the unruly curls above my ears. He glanced again at the red scrapes on my knuckles.

"And anyways, I was curious too." The kid raised his eyebrows then as if the whole thing was as obvious as a summer breeze. This was an adventure, an escapade to tell his grandchildren one day. Not a dire fix with death in the last round.

Whip took a seat on the bed and tipped his head toward Herb to finish the explanation. "This evening, when you quit the camp, you let me follow you. That was way weird. Like you were lonely and wanted to get caught. But then, when your girlfriend showed at Lonnie's Diner, I knew everything was alright. You wouldn't hurt me with your woman around, would you?"

Relying on animal instinct or intuition or just the limited imagination of youth, he had read me, sussed out my relationship with Brina in a glance. This kid's faith overwhelmed and humbled me. It was fantasy, but I wanted Whip's fairy-tale beliefs to come true.

"Didn't Eddie tell you about me? I left my card."

"Yeah, he did. I got your card that first day. But Eddie's story was kinda whack." A shrug and another scrabble under Herb's chin cranked the purring into third gear. "I couldn't make out which parts were true. And which parts he invented to get me to stop worrying."

"So that's why you didn't look me up right away? You didn't trust Eddie's report?"

"He tried his best. But I wanted to scope you for myself. So, I waited a while. Then I followed you to Lonnie's. And the rest is history." Whip's laughter rang across the apartment, the surprise sound causing Herb to leap out of his arms.

"What's your cat called? You got a dog too? Does your foot hurt all the time? Or just when you walk a lot? You got a special shoe? You use a cane or a crutch? Or just limp along like that? Where you keep your gun? You got brass knucks? Or those cool ninja num-chuks?"

Whip fired the barrage of questions without pause or aim. Like a teen at a carnival showing off for his date, hoping to hit the revolving ducks. "What you got to eat in this joint? I'm hella hungry. Aren't you?"

The kid's blithe tone spooked me. She seemed oblivious to the danger around her. She wasn't dim-witted; her survival on the streets proved otherwise. But she was brimming with such remarkable optimism that this certainty spilled over into bravado. Whip believed things would go her way simply because she willed it so. I'd been this thoughtless once, this buoyant and free. Before life–and my reckless choices—knocked the confidence out of me.

As I gathered a breath to object to Whip's fool attitude, a soft thump rattled the front door. Brina swept into the apartment, loaded with bags of takeout from Lucky No. 1, our favorite Chinese restaurant. She brought enough beef Szechuan-style, Moo Goo Gai Pan, shrimp fried rice, Buddha's Delight, and egg rolls for the three of us. And the rest of the platoon.

I wasn't much of a party host. Two plates, four forks, and a tattered package of cocktail napkins exhausted the supplies in my pantry. Leaving the food in its original containers was our best play. After I made formal introductions, Whip took a place at the foot of my bed next to Brina. I sat in front of them on the high-backed armchair. We passed the cartons in a circle until we defeated our hunger.

As we ate, Whip chattered about his work as a foot soldier in the vast financial scheme that now threatened him. He was the chief of a street brigade of twenty teens of both sexes. Their base of operation was the homeless camp, although not all members of the cashing crew lived there.

"And who was the dude you met this evening at the diner?" Brina didn't have a name for the thug.

Whip answered around a mouthful of egg roll. "That's Link. His full name is José Abraham Lincoln Ruiz, can you believe it?"

"Yeah, some handle." I liked "Missing Link" better, but nobody asked me.

"Can't blame him for cutting it short, right? Link's cool, though. He's older, twenty or twenty-two. He really knows what's going on and how to deal on the street, no matter what the situation." Even with his mouth full, the kid's lip curled into a smile and his eyes dimmed, as if star dust had blown across them. This crush thing with Link was serious, no doubt about it.

I wanted to fill in the missing puzzle pieces before we sank into the cuddly pillow of hero worship. "So, it's Link who posts the signal for your crew? He's the one who moves the flowerpot, right?"

Surprise widened Whip's eyes. I rose a few notches on his yardstick of respect. Not bad for an old geezer with a limp. "That's right. How'd you know that?"

"I got a complaint from the lady who owns the flowers. Saw Link doing some gardening, and I figured it was a signal of some kind. How's it work?"

"I receive orders from a dude named Kehinde, who hands me a deck of prepaid debit cards. When I'm told to distribute them to my team, I get Link to move the flowerpot. That way team members learn where to meet up."

Whip planted his fork in the fried rice carton to illustrate the moves. "If the flowers are at the front of the porch on the left side, it means one street corner. If they are at the back of the porch near the door, it means the other spot. Pretty cool, hunh?"

"Yeah, pretty cool." I didn't tell Whip the story of the Watergate scandal. His world was tough enough without more disillusionment.

Whip explained that when his crew arrived at the meeting spot, he distributed the doctored debit cards. He said some of his gang recruited older brothers with cars to the cause; others boosted a vehicle when needed. Kehinde told them the appointed hour when the balance limits and withdrawal limits on each debit card would be raised by computer hackers operating at secret sites around the world.

Brina whistled under her breath, prompting Whip to interrupt his narrative to complain: "That was Kehinde who tried to grab me tonight. Now why'd he want to go and do that? I never did him no harm. I was handing him the money in the backpack, just like always, but then he goes and grabs me."

She glanced at the heavy satchel under the table, then threw a soft look my way. Not as sweet as the ones she'd been shooting at Brina, but nice all the same. "If you hadn't come along, I don't know what would've happened. You messed him up big time. Pow! Pow! Kablooey!"

Whip balled his fists and threw a mighty right hook, then a left upper cut, then another right. Smiling at his good fortune, Whip continued describing his part in the heist operation. On the night of each strike, Kehinde contacted him by cell phone with the locations of dozens of ATM machines across the city. At Whip's orders, the crew fanned out waiting for word to spring into action. When he sent them the one-word text message, his friends withdrew thousands of dollars from these hacked accounts, stuffing the cash into their backpacks as they moved through the streets.

At the end of the spree, Whip's cashing crew would bring their bulging satchels to a designated drop point, where Kehinde would take the money and disappear. The following morning, he would give Whip a single backpack filled with money to distribute among the crew as their payment for services rendered.

"How much did you make?" I tried to keep my voice even and tensed my jaw to keep from gaping like a fool. I was supposed to be the adult in the room. At least one of them.

"On four nights in May and June, my cashing crew made about five hundred withdrawals. We took at least two hundred thousand dollars each night."

"Were you the only ones running this game?"

"I don't know if there were other street crews like mine. But I bet there were. I got the feeling Kehinde had more crew chiefs than just me reporting to him."

Whip leaned forward as if sharing a big secret. She tapped a finger against her temple. "I'm not so sure Kehinde is all that smart. I mean, could he really come up with this whole scheme by himself? Doubt it. Lots of muscle, but mostly between his ears. I figure there's got to be people above him, smarter and tougher than he is. But I never met anybody but Kehinde."

I agreed with Whip about the scope and complexity of the financial scam he was mixed up in. Norment Ross had described the federal investigation into the ATM theft and vast money laundering scheme; my mind was jumping double-time to keep track of all the angles in this case.

But I wanted to bring the story down to the neighborhood level. "And why did you give money to Friends In Deed? That *was* you, wasn't it?"

Whip nodded, his face shinning with true pride of accomplishment. "Dr. Sondra and Miss Keisha are the bomb. They were good to me and my mom when we first came to the shelter. They helped us tons, so I wanted to help them back."

"But you knew you were skimming from this big heist, didn't you?"

She shrugged and swiped the back of her hand across greasy lips. I threw a crumpled cocktail napkin. She wiped and continued. "I figured no one would miss the little bit I was taking. And the people at Friends In Deed could really use the money. Anyway, it's sort of a special place; it's where Link and I met."

Rust deepened the color of his cheeks at this intimate revelation. The settlement house didn't hold only bad memories for him. Why hadn't he mentioned his mother except in passing? I wasn't going to open that wound. Not until he was ready.

"So, I figured it was right to do something good for them after all they did for me and my mom. Kinda of repay them, you know. I took those selfies to polish up the money so it wouldn't seem so crude. Make it more personal."

He looked at Brina for her approval. Maybe Whip thought a woman would have more sympathy for his story than I would. He was right. I was a romantic, but the disappointed kind. I'd seen enough of the cracks and raw deals in the world to be suspicious of gentler sentiments when they came rushing at me. Softer feelings scabbed over by rude experience: that's what I'd gained on my journey from fourteen to forty.

Brina gave him the approval he craved, smiling as she gathered up the empty cartons. "It'll be alright, Whip. We'll figure out something."

Her words sounded like empty comfort, but I didn't say anything to deflate Whip's self-assurance. If he continued to trust me, things would work better for us all. Flailing and hesitancy could get us killed.

———————

I had a half-empty, semi-nasty carton of Neapolitan ice cream in the freezer. There'd be enough for the three of us, if I scraped off the top crust. But I only owned two aluminum bowls. One of them was on the floor in front of the oven holding the crumbs of Herb's dinner chow. To tackle the tri-color dessert, we needed a new, bowl-free, seating arrangement. Our conversation had been long enough and intimate enough that sprawling on the bed didn't seem as awkward as it might have been. So, we three sat on the bed side by side, backs against the headboard, with Brina squeezed in the middle.

As the ice cream shuttled from one end of the line to the other, our talk took a mellow turn. Whip spoke about early hopes to live as a boy, grow into a man. How he'd determined to grab the best life he could, even if it meant defying his mother. How he'd decided to run away and make a new life for himself, free from all those expectations that tied him to a body he didn't recognize or want. He told of wandering into the homeless camp and meeting Eddie the Pauper. Of Eddie's kindness and the patient guidance he gave in those first months when times got rough.

"It's not weird modeling my life after a homeless guy, is it?" Whip licked a dab of strawberry ice cream from the spoon and tapped it against her lower lip.

I offered a flickering glimpse into my own past. "Well, yeah, maybe. Just a little. But you could do worse. A lot worse. I did, that's for sure." Melancholy, but true. I stared at the ditch I was digging into the chocolate side of the ice cream. When I didn't say more, Brina leaned her shoulder into mine. That nudge felt like a demand for her chance at the dessert. And a little push of loving comfort in my direction. I swallowed the gob of chocolate and the sad memories melted into silence.

Brina rallied us to a lighter mood then, talking about the neighborhood detective business. She spiced the account with funny stories about her dad's love for baseball, dancing, and mechanical inventions. All the cases she remembered turned out great and nobody ever got hurt. No murders, no disappearances, no divorces, betrayals, or prison time. The tales she spun weren't pure fantasy, but mighty close.

Then it was my turn. I told stories about picking apples in Washington state, oranges in California, and pecans in the hill country of West Texas. I underlined the fun, mischief, and hard work, hinting at other stories too raunchy to tell in mixed company. I left out the army, my dead buddy, and my long-gone wife. No need to puncture our fairy tales with reality.

Ice cream done and stories wrapped, Whip scooted her feet toward the end of the bed, so her crown pressed against the headboard. Her words came slower, energy flagging at last. I doused the overhead light and we settled into a companionable silence, Brina and me sitting upright while the kid tried to sleep.

But Whip wasn't quite through. "I want to give back the money, Rook. The money in my backpack and what's left of the cash I gave at the shelter. I can go collect it tomorrow. That dough's caused too much trouble." His strawberry-sweet whisper wavered over the bed sheets pulled to his chin. "Can you help me give it back?"

I gentled my voice in the darkness. "I don't see how that would make a difference now. What's done is done."

"But I could show good will by giving it back. To whoever it was stole it."

"True, you could, Whip. But right now, we don't even know who to give it to."

She didn't say anything for such a long while I thought she'd fallen asleep. But then I heard a mewling noise, soft and low like a stunned animal caught in a trap. "That boy that got shot in the park, he was Zaire. He was my friend."

Whip hiccupped over a sob. "Good kid, but he always moved too slow. That bullet was meant for me. Zaire shouldn't have caught it. Should've been me. I was the one dragged him into this. It should've been me got shot."

Another wet moan, this time clogged deep in the chest. I didn't say I knew Zaire too. I couldn't let him go to sleep with the image of that grisly death in his head. "No, you need to stay alive, Whip. You've got a new life now. A chance to make a fresh start. That's what you're here for now."

His quiet weeping continued for another minute or two, then tapered off into rhythmic snuffling.

My chest tightened. Whip had done me a kindness simply by falling asleep in my bed. This troubled kid took a little drop of comfort from my presence beside him. I squeezed Brina's hand where it lay on the mattress between us and that eased the ache in my heart.

I couldn't see our way out of this, not yet. Whip had betrayed the code that stitched together someone's profitable financial scam, and now those powerful forces wanted him to pay. Maybe with his life. But Whip seemed confident in me and so did Brina. I was soothed by her silent presence and longed to hug her to my chest. Yearning strummed a familiar beat in me. I wanted her, as always, this constant desire pumping through me even now.

But we were on the job. Duty as much as modesty restrained me. So, instead I leaned my head against the wall. I was tired. With the room silent, all those scratchy thoughts and coiling emotions that threatened to swamp me in the daylight escaped in the stuttering sigh of a simple question. "Where'd you ditch the car?"

"In a public garage in a galaxy far, far away. Don't worry about it. When they tow it for non-payment in a few weeks, it'll be lost in the depths of the city parking authority forever." Brina sighed, pressing her fingers on my shoulder. "Aren't you sleepy?"

I didn't want to sleep. Couldn't. I was on duty, couldn't abandon the job, though my head throbbed with fatigue. I wanted to argue, wanted to make the words obey and come out in whole sentences. "No sleep..." But they skittered away. "Save Zaire..." And wouldn't be tamed.

Brina was right, as usual. "Time to stand down, soldier." She sounded firmer, her words a command guiding me where I longed to go. I sank into the mattress until I stretched flat, my face pressed into her hip. I flung my arm across her lap, then shifted so my palm rested flat against her stomach.

She hummed the first bars of "Taps," the army lullaby: "Day is done/ Set the sun..." Her warm hand stroked the hair at my temple, laying down a gentle pattern. Brina's silky voice curled through my mind. "You need to sleep now. The fight comes to us tomorrow."

CHAPTER
FOURTEEN

The bed was cold. Syrupy daylight spread from the yellow curtains, splashing on the floor.

"Brina." Eyes closed, I reached across the flat coverlet. "Brina." She should have been there.

"She's gone." Whip sat on the high-backed chair, munching shrimp fried rice, long legs propped on the bed, bare toes wriggling. She was buried in one of my white t-shirts. A giant pair of my boxer shorts draped around her like a blue-and-gray striped circus tent. "She said to tell you she had to get going. Something about work and blah, blah, blah, you know. She'll be in touch later."

I scrubbed my hands across my face to push sleep from protesting eyes. I had nothing to say to Whip's message, so she pressed on. "And she said you should go down to the laundry room and get my clean clothes out the dryer. Pronto. She tricked me. When I went for a shower, she stole my stuff. Threw me your *ginormous* underwear to put on. As *if.*"

Whip plucked at the fly of the boxers, lifting it away from her body. When I didn't say anything, she zipped me a dirty look. "I want my clothes back, man. Is Brina always this tricky? Does she pull stunts like this on you too?"

"Kinda. Yeah." Real conversation required work. Without coffee, simple syllables were all I could risk. Closed eyes smothered the confusion.

But not the kid's mouth. "She even took my sneakers." The chuckle said he admired Brina's sass. Since I did too, I didn't answer. While stealing Whip's stuff, she'd fed Herb and made coffee for me, a nice peace offering. I stumbled to the kitchen, keeping my back to Whip. A clean mug, a wobbly pour. After three gulps of black gold, I re-joined the human race.

As my head cleared, Whip pushed his case. "You gonna call her? Dude, I need my clothes!" Persistent like a fungus.

"Coffee. Shower. Then Cheerios." I turned toward the bathroom to make good on my self-instructions. "That's the order. Got it, kid?"

Pursing his mouth, Whip hiked the boxers over his slim hips and dug into the fried rice again.

The shower was cold, the soap gritty, the towels soaked, the tiles slippery. There was a reason I lived alone: sharing was its own punishment. Especially with a sloppy kid as the ungrateful roommate. When I returned to the bedroom in unbuttoned jeans, a clammy towel slung around my neck, Whip had confiscated my bowl for her own cereal.

I dug through my dresser for a clean t-shirt, her resentful gaze flaying my back. I tossed a question over my shoulder. "You going to sulk all morning?"

"No. Only until I get my clothes back."

When I didn't answer, Whip launched the attack she'd been planning since daybreak. She'd figured out my weaknesses and laced into me with a sparkle in her eye. "What's the deal with you and Brina? She's your boss? *And* your girlfriend? *And* she's a grown woman working for her daddy?"

"Yes." If I stayed shut, maybe he'd quit while I was still ahead.

"That's seriously messed up, man. She's a grown-ass woman, old enough to be on her own, making a life for herself. Last night, she talked lots about her daddy, but didn't tell any stories about her momma. What happened to *her*?"

"Disappeared when Brina was a little girl." Direct questions got a direct answer from me, always.

When I didn't elaborate, Whip let a soft whistle leak past his teeth. "Her mom ran out on her?"

"Yes. Just vanished." The gravel in my voice wasn't only from sleep's remnant grit.

"Disappeared. Rough way to lose your mom." He shook his head, then spooned more cereal into his mouth. "So Brina never learned how to be a grown woman, did she? Just made it up as she went along. Right?"

The kid had a good grasp on a convoluted situation, maybe even a better understanding than I did. I'd never pushed Brina on these questions, letting silence shroud this, as so many other topics between us. Maybe Whip's difficult relationship with his own mother gave him a big dose of cynical insight.

But conceding the point about Brina felt like betrayal, so I stayed neutral. "I don't know about that."

"So, how's that whole thing work for you? Brina and her dad both your bosses?" Whip leaned back in the chair, right foot propped on the bulging backpack on the floor.

"Yes, they run the agency."

"She's the boss in the office." Whip tilted his head toward the rumpled bed. "But *you're* the boss here, am I right?" A smirk lifted the left corner of his mouth around a shovelful of Cheerios.

I held up my right hand and started counting with the thumb: "One, not your business." Then index finger: "Two, it's complicated." I held the solo middle finger in the air for a long while: "And three, not your goddamned business."

I tried to erase the chuckle from my voice, but failed. Whip laughed until milk dribbled down his chin. Pushing adults to the limit was tons of fun. He shook his head in pity. "You're in a truckload of trouble, man."

"How d'you figure?"

"Brina's the princess in this sweet set up."

I didn't have a snappy answer, so I kept quiet. Pouring another cup of coffee was good cover.

Armed with teenage superiority, Whip had us all figured out and didn't need my prompt to unspool the analysis. "She's beautiful, smart, the prize in her daddy's eye. The whole kingdom loves the princess. So, you know what that make you in this fairy tale, don't you? There's only two roles open."

"How's that?" Not playing dumb. I really didn't know where he was going with this, but his bright eyes kept me engaged.

"Look, man, here's how it lays. Either you're the prince in disguise. Riding to save her at the last minute." In the long pause a cloud drifted across his expression.

I prodded: "Or?"

Muscles along his jaw clenched over words he didn't want to say. "Or you're the fire-breathing dragon. Got to be slayed at the end of the story to save the princess."

"Who says Brina needs saving?" Coffee burned my tongue, so the words came out garbled.

Whip hiked his shoulders, hoisting a burden children shouldn't have to carry. "It's just how the story goes. Dragon breathes fire. Prince rides in. Dragon gets slayed. Same story, every time. It's how it goes. Always has. Always will."

I shook my head and set the mug on the counter next to the milk carton. I moved to the end of the bed and smoothed the comforter to sit down. Whip's feet were crossed on the bed, so I clasped a bare ankle in my hand. The soft skin was covered in an ashy veil over delicate bones. I leaned close.

"Not always, Whip. The old story doesn't have to go the way it used to." I squeezed the thin ankle, until she glanced up. "Look at you. You're re-writing the story of your life. Breaking the rules. Telling the tale your own way. Maybe me and Brina are too. Maybe we're all making a new ending to this story."

A shadow drifted across her brown face, pressing a wrinkle between deep-set eyes. The bone structure, voice, gawky hands reminded me of Leola Covington. So, I drove the conversation to the sensitive place it needed to go. "Whip, your mother cares about you. A lot."

"You don't know that." His tongue stuck to the top of his mouth as the dry words snapped.

"I do. I met her."

He sat upright, snatching his feet from my grasp. Urgency or fright drove his voice higher. "What! Where?"

"At Friends In Deed. Last week."

"What did you tell her about me?"

"Nothing."

"What did she say?"

"She misses you."

He raised a palm toward my face and snorted: "Yeah, like a lip misses a canker sore."

"She's worried, Whip. She's your mother."

"Not my fault she ended up with me." He folded thin arms across his chest.

I pushed against his defiance. "She doesn't see it like that."

He tightened his arms, like leather straps fastened around a suitcase. His mouth opened over a wail. "You don't know what she said to me. How she looked when she said it. She *hates* me!"

"She wants to see you now." Truth was simple, delicate, and tough to take.

"No way. You're bullshitting me." When I shook my head, Whip insisted. "You working for her? Tracking me down for her? You her paid private snitch?"

"No."

"Then who you working for?" Anger and fear wrestled with curiosity in the new question.

Now was the right time, so I spilled more truth. "Zaire was my friend too. I'm working for him."

Whip pressed into the chair, curving her torso into a protective comma, knees against her chest. She shook her head again. "Unh-unh. Money talks. Zaire's not paying you."

"Doesn't matter. He was my friend, and somebody killed him. I'm going to find out who. I'm working for Zaire now. And for you."

Whip nodded, then sniffed. She might have let a tear drop, but the rude buzz of my cell phone broke our communion.

Brina's harsh squawk forced me to hold the phone two inches from my ear. Something was wrong. Dead wrong. A shrill blizzard of words surged in the air. I barked at the phone: "Slow down, Brina! What's going on?"

"*Get over here, Rook!*" Brittle distress penetrated the garble. "*Get here!*"

"You in the office?"

"*Get here now! Do it!*" She hung up. I stumbled to the bathroom looking for my shoes.

Brina rarely panicked; her head was as cool as the gun she strapped in her side holster. As I tugged the laces, Whip whined about her clothes again, pleading with me to retrieve them from the laundry room before I left. "You keeping me your prisoner? You can't do that. It's against the law."

I didn't deny the charge. She was safer in custody than roaming the streets. This kid's plea shriveled beside the danger Brina faced. Fear sharpened my orders. "Eat whatever's in the fridge. Don't open the door unless it's me or Brina. I'll call you later. Got it? You don't move until I say so."

"No!" Whip howled as I hit the door. "Wait! You can't…" The slam covered the rest of her cry. Without clothes, Whip was trapped like the enchanted royal in the legend. My apartment was no fairy-tale castle, but this gimcrack spell would hold her until I rescued Brina.

The six-block walk to the agency office usually took twenty minutes. Spurred by fear, my fast hobble shaved it to fourteen. When I pushed the glass door of our suite, I didn't know what to expect. Cops, panicky clients, furious Norment Ross. Nowhere on my list was a battered, bleeding Odette, princess of the Palace.

CHAPTER
FIFTEEN

Odette stood ramrod straight in the reception area, lips bruised and swollen, red jewels of blood scattered across her dress front. Her long sky-blue skirt was ripped from the bodice, threads dangling like white tentacles over the dark skin of her exposed waist. Her knuckles were scraped and split. A thin red scratch crawled from her right ear to below the sequined neckline, pointing to a piece of paper fixed to her collar with a safety pin.

"Odette, where's Brina?"

The old woman shook her dreadlocks, her eyes rolling from side to side as if searching the walls for an answer. "Who's Brina? I come looking for you."

Odette was about to burst into another of her idiot songs, when Brina emerged from the break room, a mug in one hand. No wounds visible, forehead and hands undamaged. Only the round eyes and trembling voice revealed undissipated tension. "Right here, Rook. Fixing tea. She turned down coffee."

"Tea for two. You get a boy and I get a girl. Two for tea." Odette's musical footnote amped the absurdity of the scene.

"What's going on, Brina?" I didn't expect Odette to give me better than nonsense, so I turned my back on her.

Brina trimmed the frills from the story, speaking about Odette as if she wasn't there. Which was true in a way. "She arrived thirty minutes ago, shrieking and calling for you. Her dress torn and bloody like this. I wrestled her into the bathroom and took a washcloth to her face. Even managed to dab a little ointment on the cut on her neck. Got her to calm down enough so she quit wailing. She kept saying she wanted to see you. That's when I phoned you."

I turned to Odette for details, as many as her fuzzy mind could produce. I gripped her elbow and steered her toward my office. She winced at my rough tug but kept her lips shut. In front of the desk, she dropped on to the couch and started stroking its leather seat like she was in a petting zoo. Brina placed the mug of tea on the lip of my desk and, stooping to catch Odette's eye, pointed at it. Odette ignored her, so with a nod at me Brina left us to our conversation.

"Tell me what happened, Odette. Can you do that?"

Shifting the folds of her dress higher on her shoulder to cover the angry scratch, she pulled an embroidered handkerchief from a hidden pocket and wiped her eyes. "I was walking, just pushing my shopping cart and walking like I do…" She gasped a sob, capturing it in her handkerchief.

"Yes, I know you do. What happened on your walk, Odette?"

"You know I walk past the diner and through the park most days. This day was the same as the others." Tears streamed down her cheeks and landed on the smooth bronze skin of her collarbones. I wanted to reach out to catch the dripping mess, but held back. Instead I sat beside her and took her damaged hand, squeezing it in both of mine. "All the neighbors know me; all the shopkeepers know me."

"Sure, they do." I nodded encouragement, trying to strike a balance between offering comfort and pressing forward with the story. I wanted to leap to the end, but Odette's addled style required a roundabout approach, even in a crisis. "Can you tell me what happened?"

"Today on my walk, two men came up to me. They jumped out of a white van. Said they needed to talk with me. It was those two men with the same face like I seen the last time in the park. They said they would give me a present after they were done. I like presents, Rook."

Her cheeks rounded into a smile. "But I'm a smart girl, too smart for that. I wasn't getting in no van with those two same-faced men. But they grabbed me and pulled me into the white van anyway."

"Did they say anything to you?" I smiled to push the story. Her pulse skittered through the gnarled veins under my fingers and set my heart racing.

Odette smacked her lips twice before answering. "They told me they had an important message and only *I* could deliver it. *Me.*" She paused to wipe her lips and eyes again.

"A message? What kind of message?" Cotton-mouth gummed my words. I took a sip from the lukewarm tea on the desk.

"Those two men, they used a safety pin to fasten a piece of paper to the collar of my dress." Odette pointed at the folded sheet on her chest. "I wrestled with them and the dress tore. Look here, the waist ripped on the left side and buttons popped off too. But they got the note pinned on me like they said they would."

"Did they hurt you?" How far did the assault go? I didn't want to know. But I needed all the facts she could bear to give, so I'd press until she stopped me.

"These men knew where I lived. They drove their van right in front of the Palace. And then they pushed me out onto the sidewalk. I fell. I skinned my knees and hands. See here."

Odette touched a knee, pinching the fabric of her skirt between two swollen fingers as she spoke. She lifted the dress to expose pink patches of flesh. The damage looked like a dull paring knife had scraped the skin from her knobby brown joints. Red hashmarks scored her palms.

"You need to let Brina help you clean those knees."

"Who's Brina?" Eyes careened to the aluminum blinds then the file cabinets in the corner. "She your girl?"

"Yes, that's her. She brought you the tea."

"Nice girl, Rook. Real nice. Pretty. You did good." Odette pressed a hand to her mouth and then to her flat chest. But the approval in her words didn't rise to her eyes. They glowed with grief, shock, and some other emotion. Maybe accusation.

"Why didn't they come to you direct? They should have come to you, Rook. Not me." Odette raised both hands as if holding a crown over her head, then pressed them against her scalp. She gripped locks in both fists like she intended to jerk the matted hair out by the roots. "They asked me did I know a man named Rook. I said I did. They asked me if I knew where you were. Then they told me to bring the message to you. Why send *me* with their note?"

We were in the dark. The befuddled leading the blind. But she looked to me for answers as we stumbled together. She held the hem of her dress at arm's length, the ripped waistband gaping. Brick red spots of dried blood marked the skirt's frayed hem.

"I don't know, Odette. I don't know."

"Look what those men did to my beautiful party dress. They didn't take my necklace." She pulled the chain from her bodice and caressed the purple stone of the little gold ring Eddie had given her. "But my beautiful blue dress. Tiffany blue. So gorgeous. Look at it." She lifted the folds of her skirt, thrusting the bloodstained pleats toward me as mute evidence of the attack.

"I see it, Odette. I promise you this. They'll pay for this. You have my word. They'll pay for what they've done."

Odette nodded, her story finished. But for one detail, the contents of the note. The message was the key to the matter. My stomach clutched in dread. "Let me see the note."

Odette straightened her shoulders and fiddled with the paper at her collar. The page was a white half-sheet of heavy stock, folded in quarters, its creases sharp, the metal safety pin glittering in one corner. The pin's clasp defied her numb fingers, so I pushed them aside and took the paper.

———

I helped Brina plaster Odette with Band-Aids on every limb, and antiseptic on every scratch. When she was patched up, I added two fingers of bourbon to sweeten her tea.

She swallowed the mix, then a second dose, straight, no tea. Fortified and talkative again, Odette begged to be driven to the Palace. As a formality, I offered to help her file a police report of the attack. That was never going to fly. In her view, a brush with the cops would make the assault by these thugs seem like a Coney Island Ferris wheel ride. So Brina and I drove Odette toward her home.

We crawled through sluggish midday traffic, the stench of tar and gasoline fumes rising between bumpers. Dripping brown arms pumped threats through open windows, hot voices promised mayhem in five languages. Jerk, stop, dart, stop. Rev, halt, jerk. Our juddering pace mimicked the brute words of the message Odette had delivered with such pain: *Meet. Alone. Suffer.* The typed note was a summons from Martin Colón, Harlem's top mobster. His message clear and menacing:

"PI Rook—Meet 8 tonight—North end Bronx Swamp—Alone or your family suffers—Don't show and your family suffers–Colón"

I knew Martin Colón, but only to squint at. I'd met him on one occasion, a birthday party for his granddaughter eight months earlier. His daughter had hired the Ross Agency as discreet muscle to stop her ex-husband from ruining the child's celebration. At the time, I had no idea who Colón was; he looked like a pudgy old papi with thick black mustachios and a jovial air. He was happy with my service and gave me a few hundred dollars as a tip for the job.

After our brief meeting, Norment Ross filled me in: Martin Colón ran all major crime operations in the borough: drugs, loan sharking, extortion, gambling, prostitution. Getting Norment to spill about his connection to the gangster was a struggle. Nostalgia played no part in the memories. In those bad old days, Norment had been a numbers runner for Colón when they hung with a crowd of rising baby thugs. Norment's description of the man chilled like dry ice: "Martin Colón is a good man to know. And a good man to avoid. Anything you come across in this neighborhood, if it stinks, Martin has his hand on it. You name anything rotten, twisted, or corrupt, Martin Colón's behind it."

Now the gang boss had his hands on me.

The purpose of the proposed meeting was clear. Whip's green backpack crew was right in the middle of this. If the money Whip was skimming belonged to a big-time mob chief like Colón, then the trouble we faced was foul, greasy, and disastrous for our health.

We didn't drive as far as Odette's warehouse. One block from the Palace, she spotted her metal shopping cart. She demanded we let her out to reclaim her property. On the sidewalk, the old woman caressed the handle of her battered wagon, then fingered her stacks of fabric and magazines, counting to make sure every precious scrap and edition was unscratched.

As Brina cranked out a U-turn, she asked the simplest question facing us. "Think she'll be okay?"

"We did what we could. I'll check on her tomorrow." Abrupt, not rude. Other problems pressed for answers. Tightened fingers on the steering wheel was Brina's only response.

She left the next round of questions to me. "Right now, I need to get ready for Colón's tea party tonight. What do you know about the Bronx Swamp?"

I'd never heard of the place, but Brina's description struck cold: "It stinks. Literally."

"I can leave my white gloves and high heels at home?"

"And your smart-ass attitude too." No coddling smiles from Brina. She stared through the pollen-streaked windshield at the passing traffic. "The Bronx Swamp is a mile-long stretch of derelict rail line. Conrail abandoned it fifteen years ago because its tight curves and low tunnel under St. Mary's park made it impossible for modern freight cars to pass."

"Is it a real swamp? With banjo-picking alligators and in-bred mutants?"

Brina wasn't having my jokes. She continued her account of the dump through gritted teeth. "Just a water-logged sinkhole. The city tried to drain it a few times, but then they threw up their hands and the Bronx Swamp stayed a boggy mess."

"Have you seen it? Up close?"

"I've driven by a few times. A cop I know in the 40th Precinct told me the underpass is mainly a collection of rotting cross ties, putrid water, and decades of neighborhood trash."

"Sounds like I need a passport and a tetanus shot to get into this party." I made light of the threat to keep Brina from worrying. I couldn't stop her feelings. She'd want to provide back-up. She'd be damn good at it too. But this had to be a one-man mission.

As we idled at a red light, she inhaled to make the offer. I cut her off before she spit out the words. "I go this alone, Brina. You saw the note: '*Alone or your family suffers.*'"

"I read it. I'm not scared. Not one bit."

"I know you're not. But if you came along, *I'd* be scared." Staring through the side window kept my emotions to a low boil.

"Then take my weapon. You need to be armed going against Colón's gang."

"If I take a gun, I double the chances of getting shot before the night ends. I don't need the added risk. Trust me: I got this."

Brina was going to out-tough-guy me on this. No rant or tears, only a ripple in the clenched muscles of her jaw bared her feelings. She curbed her concerns with the trust I relied on. She was willing to let me play the match as I saw it. Reading this dangerous game right was my best bet.

Don't show and your family suffers.

Colón threatened Brina and Norment. They counted as family. But was the circle wider? Were Whip and his mother and the ladies of Friends In Deed at risk too? Odette had already suffered. Maybe her consort Eddie was in the crosshairs now as well.

The gangster intended to inflict damage as widely as he could across our neighborhood, using terror to achieve his criminal aims. If I could intercept him now, as he expanded his power through a sophisticated computer scam, maybe I could thwart him. I had no illusions about how effective I could be. At best, I was a speck of grit in his machine. I couldn't hope to stop it altogether.

But maybe the Colón organization wasn't an impersonal engine at all. Maybe it was something more organic, a living creature. A writhing octopus in its crib with clammy tentacles wrapped around my wrist, squeezing until the veins bulged. But if I choked hard enough, maybe I could stunt the life of Colón's gang in its infancy.

This Bronx Swamp appointment with Colón had to be a solo job, a lightning strike without back-up. No alternative worked. I'd tackle the operation alone, damn the risk.

CHAPTER
SIXTEEN

Martin Colón's idea of a rendezvous spot reeked.

The tunnel's vault spewed the smells of mold, decay, and rot from a dozen mammal carcasses into a putrid fog over the neighborhood. The cloying stink slapped my face. By the time I reached the overpass, I wished I'd worn long sleeves to cover my nose.

The taxi dropped me on a street bordering St. Mary's Park and I walked the three blocks to the viaduct that overhung the Bronx Swamp. A derelict shirt factory and an abandoned tool works plant witnessed my trek through the unfamiliar neighborhood.

In the office, I'd changed into a black t-shirt and replaced my sneakers with heavy boots. I stowed a cheap switchblade in the back pocket of my jeans and a sturdy knife in the shaft of the right boot. I left my cell phone and wristwatch in the desk drawer. Before these preparations, I'd sent Brina to my apartment with two meatball subs as a peace offering to Whip. I said I'd meet her later. She'd grumbled, but agreed Whip needed protection, so she took the guard duty shift.

Now, I clambered down the incline from the street at the north end of the railway underpass, hanging on to naked branches as I descended. I hesitated at a seven-foot high retaining wall. Jump and risk twisting an ankle or dangle from the concrete overhang to make the shorter fall to the uneven ground below. I dropped from the wall, landing on a pile of bricks and a garbage can cover. My bum foot squawked, but I ignored the complaint.

Glinting in the shadows of the underpass was a pearl-gray Escalade, headlights extinguished, motor humming. Acrid fumes poured from its exhaust, blending with the fruity stench of decayed wood.

As I walked toward the vehicle, three figures slid from the shadows on either side of the SUV. Two of the men were in their mid-twenties. They were tall and lean, with skin shaded deep walnut and plum black. I recognized the third man: older than his comrades, he had the scowling face and stocky build of the crew chief Kehinde. I nodded to acknowledge the reunion, but he stared at me with blank eyes. Maybe my fist in his mug hadn't left such a memorable impression after all.

The men dressed in somber colors with a quasi-military air. Their hair styles were close cropped; the man I thought was Kehinde wore a high top with shorn sides, while another's balding scalp shone in the scant moonlight.

I spoke first in case they thought I was intimidated. "Where's your boss? He wouldn't get his feet wet down here until he was sure I'd come alone. Am I right?"

They said nothing. I advanced, stepping around a stained mattress and several wooden crates, the slats sticking up at precarious angles. I kicked at the remnants of a rotten rail tie. Splinters skittered to the feet of a man in a navy vest.

Still in charge, I kept talking. "Classy digs you got here. The Colón gang really knows how to throw a party, hunh?"

The man with the high top swiveled his drawn gun at me. When I was beside him, his pal in navy patted me with rough strokes, grunting when he found the little switchblade in my back pocket. He showed it to High Top.

"Fool was packing, Tai. Whatchu want me to do with it?"

So, this Tai resembled Kehinde, but wasn't him. The violent look-alikes of Odette's muddled story were identical twins. Tai shrugged, seized the knife, and turned his eyes toward the SUV's blank windshield. He tipped his head to the right, like a dog waiting for a command.

"Get in here." The order from the vehicle rolled hollow and deep, a rumble so muted I wasn't sure I'd heard anything at all. But the three men jumped at the sound. They fell aside, creating a path to the Cadillac's left rear door.

I climbed in and waited in silence as my eyes adjusted to the dark interior. Smoky sandalwood blended with the softer smells of baby powder and new leather in the close atmosphere of the SUV.

Colón was not quite as I remembered him. I'd imagined a soft-bellied man with loose jowls under his black moustache and the manicured hands of a bank vice president.

But the man slumped next to me on the rear bench of the SUV was well-muscled and strong. Beside black sideburns, his brass cheeks showed a faint shadow. The dark pouting lips pursed small within the curve of his thick jaw. His eyes, when he turned them on me, were small too, glowing coals behind round glasses. His curved shoulders and lowered head made him seem shy. His hands were a pickpocket's claws, wiry and clever. The tense clench of his fists against his belly set my nerves jangling.

"You came on time." Colón's first words carried a surprised tone, which he erased with his next phrase. "Smart move. I don't like to wait."

"I'm here. Your invitation was hard to pass up."

"I needed to get your attention and guarantee your cooperation."

"You got my attention. But I'm not guaranteeing anything. What do you want?"

Colón turned his large head and looked to the tunnel's inky cavern. "To talk."

"So, talk. Or are you waiting for an even bigger audience?" I thrust my chin toward the shadowy figure in the driver's seat.

The boss's face flushed, rosy pink under the brass, then a smile flashed. The glimpse of teeth made me doubt my eyesight. Had Colón blushed? Was this hint of humanity a sour trick to soften me?

"That's Crystal. My wheelman. She sticks with me. Turn around, Crystal. Let Mr. Rook meet you proper."

The woman who craned her neck to catch my eye was maybe twenty-one, small and tobacco colored with delicate snub features gashed by a sneer. Pageant-winner cute in another life. She tugged the black hood of her sweatshirt, folding it around her neck after flipping out a long glossy pony tail.

"Rook." Her voice was raspy and guarded, but confident.

"Crystal. Nice meeting you." Yeah, I was old and cranky. I jabbed at this baby gangster with a show of excess politeness. "The pleasure's all mine."

Formalities done, Colón took the lead. "I want to talk with you about that boy, girl, whatever... Whip."

Even though I'd known this was coming, my heart tilted in dread. "Whip? Who's that?"

"He's been stealing what's mine."

"What makes you think I know anything about that kid?"

"He's under your protection." Colón offered this statement as bland fact rather than a question.

I had to test the assumption. Lives depended on the challenge. "Says who? I hardly know the kid." I shifted, turning my shoulders to stare at the mob boss.

In response, he thundered a command, as if calling on a data base for elaboration of the algorithms behind the claim. "*Crystal!*"

The young woman raised her hazel eyes to catch my glance in the rear-view mirror. After a pause, she spoke without turning her head. "He lying. Kid's been holed up at his place for two days."

Crystal snapped out the charge and then launched into the explanation, her cool gaze pinned on me. "Kid hangs out in a settlement house and at a homeless camp. Rook been visiting both places, tracking the kid for a week. Yesterday, kid caught up with him and stayed all night at his crib. Most likely still there. Under Rook's protection for sure." Her lip curled in triumph. Crystal defied me to deny the conclusion.

When I remained silent, Colón seized the conversation. "You have the boy in your possession. I want to speak with him. Discuss some business we have in common."

"Kill him you mean." Interruption was the only power I had.

"I wasn't going to hurt that little brother, just give him some much-needed instruction in the way the world works." Maybe Colón didn't care about incidentals like sex or gender or identity. Power mattered. Control counted. And Whip had upset that power, bent that control.

"The world according to Martin Colón, hunh? You tried to use this kid and now he turned the tables on you. You got played by a fourteen-year-old."

Colón sucked three deep breaths to regain his composure. His flaring nostrils and fixed stare burned the air between us.

"I'm going to overlook your poor manners, Mr. Rook, as well as your ignorance of the facts." Wind labored through his thick chest, his black dress shirt tightening over jerking biceps. "When I was in seventh grade, I took art class from Mrs. Santos."

He peered at me. Would I balk at this digression? I shrugged and raised my eyebrows. No more interruptions, the stage was his to command.

"We didn't have much in the way of supplies, only what Mrs. Santos could buy with her own money–paper, charcoals, sometimes water color paints. I loved that class, I got to the studio early every Thursday all year long. I just wanted to fill every corner of every page with sketches, pictures, shapes and words. Everything I had going on in my mind I wanted to get down on that paper."

He shook his head in wonder, the excitement of those artistic hours burning in his dark eyes. Then a frown crumpled the broad expanse of his brow. "Usually my teachers ignored me. They were just happy if I stayed quiet in the back of the classroom." A snarl thrust that nasty memory into the vehicle's gloom.

"But Mrs. Santos, she encouraged me, said nice things about my drawings: imaginative, creative, gifted. Shit like that. I don't know if she meant it, but it was nice to hear anyway. Kept me going when things got bleak."

Colón's school days hadn't been so different from mine: loneliness and boredom peppered with a little bullying. The unhappy mess lifted by the presence of a few great teachers who looked inside me to draw out a morsel of value, a crumb of grace. I knew what Colón had been through because I'd been there myself.

"But then one time, Mrs. Santos said something I never forgot. She said the spaces you leave blank carry as much information as the ones you crowd with lines and images. She called it 'negative space.'" Colón stopped, his eyes growing filmy as he remembered his childhood art studio. "Negative space is like a pause between the lines of a song, making the words stand out sharp, highlighting the ideas by defining the boundaries. Negative space is the quiet, the absence that brings balance and meaning to a composition. That's what Mrs. Santos said."

Colón stopped his story and pinned me with a laser glare. "And that's what I need from your boy now: quiet absence. I need him to be the negative space around my operations. I want him to stay out of my business."

I'd been holding my breath through the art lesson. When it ended, I took the thread of the conversation. "So, you're planning to make a move in the city, are you? This bank scam is just the first step?"

Colón nodded, his eyes chilly within the wrinkles of a smile. His bushy moustache moved over white block teeth. "The old lions' days are done. They either retire gracefully or get trampled."

"And by 'gracefully' you mean the old mobsters should agree to be assassinated in quiet little restaurants on side streets in Brooklyn."

Now the moustache lifted over a full-blown smile, its bursting spark highlighting his handsome face. "Right, that would be preferable. Or they can launch an all-out war. Many of their people will get cut down in the battle. Plenty of innocent civilians too. Choice is up to them, but the outcome is certain."

Disruptions forgotten, calm again, Colón's face glowed at the prospect of a bloody confrontation with the reigning gangland kings. "If they chose to go down fighting, they will lose. No way around it. Colombians, Mexican cartel, Bulgarians. All of them gangbangers came at me. And all of them bent the knee. Now my time is dawning."

He paused, then drilled me with a dark glance. "You're smart, Rook. You can read the situation. You know the score. Join me. A man with your skills, nerve, and knowledge could go far in my organization."

He held up a hand, a fleshy stop sign pushed toward my nose. The dense mossy notes of his cologne coated my face. "Don't give me an answer now. Just think about my offer."

A grin snaked across his mouth. I was startled by this bold bid. I shifted on the bench as a whoosh of air escaped from Crystal in the front seat. She was surprised too. A dangerous thing unleashed. He'd ordered me to think only. I didn't need to answer. Yet.

I turned to the immediate question. "So, I carry this message to Whip. Tell him to back off your business. Then what?"

"I want to meet with him. Tomorrow night. I want him to bring the money. And I want you to bring him..."

"I'm not going along with any scheme like…"

"…And if you don't, I will order the boy's death tomorrow. Got it?"

It was settled. No negotiation, no play for time. Square action. I was trapped with no move, no deal. The only way out was forward. Straight into Colón's den.

"In person, Rook. You bring him to me and we'll talk."

"Now I'm your messenger boy, carrying notes. Like that old woman your men messed with this morning." A feeble gambit, but worth the bid. I didn't have another move.

"My men didn't mess with any old woman. They operate under strict orders from me. My rule is we respect girls and women like they're all our own mothers."

A sneer curled the edge of my lip. I leaned closer to the boss. I'd lost the round, but I could deliver a jab before I quit. "Your little rule got broken today, Martin. I saw the old woman's torn dress. And all that blood on her skirts was hard to miss too."

At this news, fog dimmed Colón's face. Veins at the sides of his neck bulged, and the meaty blocks of his hands clutched at his thighs. He lowered the glass on the right-side window. Without shouting, he projected his voice into the void of the black tunnel. "Taiwo, get over here!"

The lieutenant scurried into place; his high-topped head framed in the window. Kehinde's twin was as vicious as his brother. Taiwo and Kehinde were the "same-faced men" Odette had seen in the park the night of the drive-by shooting that ended Zaire's life. Their white van had brushed against Odette after our stoned corner talk. And this morning, Taiwo had dragged her into that white van to beat her with casual brutality. I wanted revenge for the murder and the assault. But I wasn't in a position to get it. Yet.

"What's up, Boss?" Taiwo's eyes darted from Colón's face to mine, trying to assess the situation.

"Tell me about that woman today. Did you touch her?"

"I pinned that note on her dress. Just like you told us, Boss. That's all."

"Did you *touch* her?"

"I never did! And that's the truth. I swear on my momma's grave."

"Don't tell me about your mother's grave, Taiwo. I know exactly how she got in it and who put her there."

I leaned forward to interrupt. An inkling of the fatal price of my claim scratched at my mind. "The torn dress, the blood, I saw it with my own eyes."

"*Crystal!*" Colón bellowed at his baby-faced driver, demanding resolution. Either Taiwo was lying or I was.

The voice from the shadows of the front seat pierced the sandalwood and smoke: "Taiwo lying."

"Deal with it."

Crystal raised her hand, slim fingers curved around a Glock. Before Taiwo could squawk a protest, the little assassin fired a single bullet through his right eye. His head bucked in the frame of the SUV's open window as the blast tore the socket. The shot ripped off a quarter of the forehead, exposing its red interior like raw meat in a butcher's shop. The dead man slumped to the ground, disappearing from the scene, his role finished.

I hadn't meant for Taiwo to die, to pay for his insult to Odette in this final manner. I'd hoped Colón would scold his lieutenant with a few harsh words. Maybe a shove or a slap across the face, as a lesson to the other thugs in his command.

But that wasn't the whole truth. I'd anticipated Colón's brutal response to my baiting from the start. If his reaction was unbalanced, that was beyond my control. I intended to cause mayhem in his organization, to disrupt the elemental bonds of trust that ran like connective tissue through the body of the mob. I wanted to rip apart the confidence Colón had in his soldiers and shred the faith they had in him. I wanted them to pay for Zaire's death.

Or your family suffers

I aimed to make his family suffer as he had mine. If I'd achieved even a small success in that effort this night, then my promise to Odette was fulfilled. And my revenge for Zaire's murder exacted a first payment.

———————

The drive from the Bronx Swamp was silent, each passenger in the pearl-gray SUV contemplating an unknowable future. Colón, coiled and grim beside me, stared at the night profile of the city. Crystal flexed short fingers on the steering wheel, jerking the vehicle through empty streets.

I didn't fear for my life or that of any one dear to me this evening. The mobster had gained what he wanted: I agreed to bring Whip to meet Colón the following night. He'd named a corner for the rendezvous and I promised to bring the satchel of money. When the SUV lumbered from the underpass, I'd thought Colón would blindfold me to cover his favored paths through the boroughs. But he scoffed at the idea.

"I'm not going anyplace you don't know, Rook. No secrets here, my operations are transparent."

Crystal jabbed the radio console until she found mellow jazz for the ride across town. Cerebral Coltrane and long, involved cuts from Thelonious Monk wafted through the SUV's interior from WBGO, The Jazz Source out of Newark. Did the musical accompaniment reflect Colón's tastes? Or those of his death-dealing driver?

After an hour of wandering, the SUV stopped beside a little park in Harlem. Colón fastened plastic ties around my wrists and ankles. "A minor inconvenience. I just want to make sure you don't get out of here too fast."

Crystal steered over the curb, across the sidewalk, and then rolled through the graveled playground, stopping near the naked skeleton of a jungle gym. Three figures hunkered at the far corner of the park, but it was otherwise empty.

"Get out." Colón was as abrupt now as he had been expansive earlier in the evening.

I obeyed, standing beside the vehicle, leaning so my chest touched its warm door. Colón's last words were clear. "You won't be stuck here long. What with that sweet knife you got hidden in your boot."

I lowered my eyes, feeling as exposed and transparent as Colón claimed to be. He swiveled his huge head to scan the playground and the dark buildings hulking at the far end of the park. "I guess you know where you are now; you can get home pretty easy from here." The gangster returned his blazing eyes to my face, lifting his chin in farewell. "Until tomorrow night, Rook. Think about my offer. And give my regards to my old friend Norment."

No smile, not even a nod. I hopped back, teetering to keep my balance. The window slid into place, and Crystal hit the gas pedal. I shivered, though the wave of air in the huge vehicle's wake was clammy with summer heat. As I watched it roll into the shadows, I reflected on this last unspoken message from Colón. I did know this place. This was the pocket park two blocks from Brina's apartment. Yards from the spot where I'd seen my friend Zaire gunned down by snipers under Martin Colón's command.

No space was sacred, no relationship off limits. The message was etched like the brute black typeface on a slip of white paper: *Or your family suffers.* The Colón mob's reach was long and its grasp dreadful and accurate.

As I bent to fish the knife from my boot, I craned my neck for a glimpse of Brina's darkened window. I braced for explanations, tough pleading, quiet anger, and perhaps a share of tears too.

The noose thrown over Whip's head cinched tight around all of us now.

CHAPTER
SEVENTEEN

When I cracked the door of my apartment, I expected to find Brina and Whip wolfing sandwiches and watching zombie soap operas on TV.

Instead, as I stood in the middle of the quiet room, Brina's hooded eyes ducked my gaze. "He was gone when I got here."

"No message? Nothing?" I inspected the uneaten meatball subs on the kitchen counter, as if their wax paper wrapping held a clue to the disappearance. "What the *hell* happened?"

Brina dropped in the armchair after wrestling a small notepad from her jeans pocket. "I don't know."

"What about the backpack, the one with all the cash he was carrying?"

"Gone too. I guess Whip took it with him when he skipped." Brina sighed, glanced again at her notes and continued. "I checked with every neighbor on this floor, asking if they'd seen or heard anything." Her fingers flew over her lists, thumping the pages with a ballpoint as she read. She rattled through names, occupations, times, and excuses. Thirteen apartments checked. Four no answers. In the other nine, no one had anything concrete to offer.

Finished with the empty interviews, Brina twisted her mouth to the side to blow a jet of air. "Then I went to the basement to check if Whip had retrieved his clothes from the laundry room. No joy." She pointed toward two stacks of clean clothing piled on the bed and smiled thinly. "Ironed and folded. At least, I accomplished something today."

"What about Mr. Greene, the super?" I sat on the bed opposite her, elbows digging into my knees. "He's zonked most of the time, but he could have caught something useful by accident."

"Yeah, I rousted him in his basement apartment. He saw zero. Knew less." She drew a line through the superintendent's name. "But when I returned to the lobby, I found a Mrs. Bustamante at the mailboxes. Retired schoolteacher, returning home from grocery shopping."

"Yeah, she lives two doors down the hall from me. Did she have anything?"

Brina nodded, two rapid jerks with her eyes still glued to the notebook. "Mrs. Bustamante said she'd heard rustling packages and crackling papers outside your door. She figured you had ordered takeout and the noise was the pizza guy making the delivery."

"She hear any voices?" I stepped to the fridge where I kept a bundle of takeout menus clipped to the door by a magnet. They were gone.

"No voices, only crumpling paper." Brina brandished the sheaf of menus, then spread them on the table next to her notepad. "I called every restaurant. Nobody had received an order from your address. No one had seen a customer matching Whip's description either."

"Christ." I sat on the bed again, pulled off both boots and stuffed my filthy socks inside. Then I stood and pitched them toward the dresser. "This is fucked up."

Brina sniffed and rose to fasten her arms around my waist. "At least, you're safe." She looked up; no tears, but purple smudged the hollows under her eyes.

I'd worried her; she didn't deserve that. Breath hitched in my chest and I hugged her. I couldn't tell her everything about the Bronx Swamp exchange with Colón yet. Maybe never. But I could share my conclusion about Colón's role in the ATM hacking scheme.

Brina jumped into that scenario with gusto. "So, he's the brains behind this whole heist gig, is he? Makes sense."

"Yes. Looks that way to me."

Brina sounded elated with this news, eager to elaborate on the scheme she saw unfolding. She paced from the table to the front door and back, her arms spread wide. "It's not hard to believe Colón has the manpower, weaponry, imagination, and greed to make this operation plausible. He's also got the international reach and computing power to bring his idea to life."

I wasn't interested in sky-high speculation. But Brina was on a tear, her words flowing in a breathless deluge. This flood of talk was her way of releasing the tension my Bronx Swamp sortie had wound so tight. So, I let her gush as she circled the room.

"If Colón's got an operation that can hack the computer systems of credit card processing companies and banks all over the world, he's perpetrating cybercrime on a vast scale. He's manipulating the entire global financial system." She sounded scared and impressed at the same time.

I would've been too, if I'd understood half of what she said. "Nothing I can do about Colón hacking the international banking system. Snake's going to slither. It's how he's made."

On my second trip to the fridge, I pried ice from a tray in the freezer, dropped the cubes in a glass, and topped them with tap water. When I'd headed for home, hunger had clutched my gut. I'd hoped Whip and Brina had saved some of the meatball subs for me. But now the craving had died. Ice water was all I could force into my surging stomach. I offered Brina a glass, but she shook it off.

I continued my take on Colón: "If he can run a fancy, tricked-out operation like this, hats off to him. It's up to other people, smarter than me, to stop his drive to be master of the universe." I could only control what happened in my little corner of the universe. And at the moment, Whip and Brina were at the center of that neighborhood. My community was small, a few square miles in a city of thousands. But the stakes were huge: lives that mattered were at risk if I failed.

As I stood at the kitchen peninsula gulping water, Brina expanded on her guesses about Colón's global empire building. She sat at the table again, her eyes gleaming with the high of discovery. The more she talked, the easier it was to avoid telling her everything else I'd learned in my exchange with the gang leader.

Everything I'd learned was ugly: the threat to Whip; the score I'd settled; the murder I'd provoked; the one-woman hit squad, the job offer I'd failed to reject. The whole corrupt web reeked worse than the garbage in that infected tunnel. The dishonesty and the snap-judgment execution were bad. But worse was Colón's casual assumption that I fit into the world he commanded. Was he right about me?

The murder of Taiwo was a test. Colón was probing, poking for weakness, posing questions I dreaded: would I recoil from the brutality or sit there and take it? Would I see the killing as justified discipline or a cold extermination? Would disgust or blood-red satisfaction color my response?

I'd passed Colón's test, for sure. I was the dragon Whip had warned me about. Whatever Colón was searching for, I guess he'd looked past my nice detective job and my nice girl and my nice Eagle Scout life to poke at something raw underneath. Colón assumed I was as corrupt as he was.

What was I supposed to do with this discovery? Let it slide off me the way rainwater swirls down gutters into the Bronx Swamp? Or could I use this new insight to advantage? Could Colón's belief that I was rotten become another weapon in my arsenal? If I worked all the angles right, maybe I could harness this. Make it work in my favor, turn Colón's assumptions against him in the fight to protect my family, my neighborhood.

Brina dragged a hand across her nose and mouth, erasing a film of sweat clouding her features. She would hate my twisted thoughts. And my decision to grip Colón's filthy proposition and turn it into a weapon. So, the outline of the plan I dropped to her was bare. A skeleton of words with no muscle or flesh. I wasn't bargaining with her. Or debating or explaining. I couldn't risk it. A design danced behind my gritty eyes, teasing hopes. Maybe I could protect Whip. If I worked all the angles. Pulled all the levers. The faint spark of an idea flickered, but it severely tested my will. If Brina mounted a sensible argument, the flame would gutter. If it was going to work, my plot required face-to-face negotiation with Colón. Without a direct appeal to him, everything would collapse. I couldn't refuse to tell Brina something, but I couldn't let her talk me out of it.

And, of course, she tried. "You going after Colón tonight was bad enough." She jerked the pen, scarring the tabletop. "Now you want to go back?"

"Yes. Not negotiable." I needed to find Whip before it was too late. His life, all of our lives, depended on finding him in time to make our twilight appointment with Martin Colón. I peeled my black t-shirt from my shoulders; the stench of the swamp swirled around my head as I threw it to the floor.

"I got this worked out, Brina." I sounded sharp, as if I knew what came next. I tossed short sentences; the ideas crisp, energy crackling through the words. As if I had all the details fine-tuned.

When I stepped out of my soiled jeans, she stared at me then released the ballpoint. She watched it roll to the edge of the table then plunge to the carpet. "I can help. I can make it work with you. Let me."

Her eagerness pressed against my bare chest like a magnet reversed, the force of her words repelling me even as she drove to connect. "Let me help you."

"I go this alone, Brina. It only works if I do." The gap between us vibrated with a tuneless hum, quivering in dark mockery as we argued.

"Why? What's your plan?" She held out her palm like a cup to share the ideas flickering in my head.

I rocked on my heels, angling away. "Trust me. I got this."

"Trust isn't the question, is it?" Withdrawing her hand, she let it fall to her side, empty.

Brina trudged to the kitchen, scrounged a black trash bag from under the sink, and unfurled it with a violent shake. She moved around the room collecting the foul clothing I'd discarded: t-shirt on the floor, socks inside my boots, stained jeans and boxers crumpled next to the bed. When the sack was full, she cinched it with a plastic tie and dumped it near the garbage can. Her mouth was tight, the cords of her neck rigid. Her dry gaze scraped the corners of the room, avoiding my eyes.

Exhausted by the events of the last few days, I retreated to a shower for relief. Zaire's murder, Link's sadistic cruelty, Colón's intrigue, Crystal's brutality, Whip's disappearance, Brina's despair. Every horror sluiced down the drain as the water streamed over my body. Muscles stretched but didn't calm; gut clenched, still aggravated and sore. I slapped the towel across my shoulders, roughed my hair, rubbed my eyes. Drops that remained on my skin chilled me enough for sleep.

I returned to a darkened room, moonlight coating the table, chair, and kitchen counters in dull pewter. Brina was already under the bed covers, legs straight, arms stiff at her side. I joined her but she didn't turn to me. I had nothing more for Brina. We'd said enough, done enough. We lay side by side like dinner knives in a cutlery tray: dull, cool, and silent.

Ten minutes, maybe more passed, punctuated by rough breathing; the cat stepped across my feet, then curled in the armchair. From the street, a siren's moan vibrated against the window pane, then stopped. In the restored silence, Brina's hair rustled on the pillow as she turned her head. Her voice drifted in puffs across my face. "I wanted to tell you something earlier."

"Tell me what?"

"I bought a pregnancy test kit yesterday."

I held my breath. "And?"

"I didn't get to use it." Her profile against the window's sheen was soft and still. "My period came today."

"Oh, Brina, why didn't you say something?" I rolled onto my side. When she began sniffling, I tucked her shoulder under my arm, her wet nose pressed against my chest.

She repeated her earlier words: "I wanted to tell you before. But everything got in the way: Whip here overnight, then Odette. Then Colón's swamp and Whip disappearing. I just couldn't find room in between."

I nuzzled the top of her head, whispering into her hair, "You okay?"

"Not yet." Her breathing hitched as her mouth moved against my skin. "But I will be."

"Okay."

"I delayed taking the test."

"Yeah, I know. Why?"

"I wanted to put off getting a concrete answer. Avoid seeing that little plus or minus sign on the stick. Keep the future undefined for a while longer. Vague and open that way, I didn't have to make a decision. And neither did you." She sighed and continued. "Now that the possibility is gone, I realize I wanted this."

"I didn't know if you did. Not for sure. I needed to hear it from you first." I squeezed her back, feeling the long muscles slide under my hands. "I wanted it too."

"I'm sorry." A sob cloaked her words.

"Nothing to be sorry about, Brina. Nothing at all."

She nodded, her brow moving against the hair on my chest. Our earlier argument set aside, we fell asleep soon after.

———————

Food. Hunger pangs jerked me awake.

Whip had to have eaten something during his captivity in my apartment. Whatever he'd scarfed might give a clue to his location. I'd told him to eat, and with my refrigerator in Mother Hubbard condition, it was easy to figure out what he'd taken. I tiptoed to the kitchen as Brina slept.

In my desperation, I tackled the fridge even before I made the morning coffee, hoping to find a clue to Whip's whereabouts in its grungy depths. Three yogurt cups were gone, as was the whole slab of Colby. The milk carton was down to its final teaspoon, so he'd gotten plenty of dairy yesterday. But those scant calories weren't near enough for a hunger-crazed teen to survive the day. Cleaning up last night, Brina had stowed the meatball sandwiches, cold and untouched in their original wrappers. A yellow paper coffee cup stood next to the sink's leaning tower of dirty dishes.

Padding into the kitchen, Herb the cat bumped his head against my ankles. He didn't care what Whip had eaten yesterday. Herb didn't care if I never had another clue or plan in my entire life. He wanted his breakfast and he wanted it now. Butting his head against my ankles had worked before, so Herb tried it again, rubbing until I obeyed. I placed the bowl of cat chow next to the trash can as always. Then I set a bowl of fresh water next to it. Herb's tail thrashed the metal bin as he bolted his breakfast. The lid was ajar. I tried to crush it closed, but the overflow resisted my push. I lifted the top to see why it wouldn't close. Stuffed under the can's lid was a large yellow sack, with napkins and wax paper crumpled inside. I pulled the bag out and set it on the counter, smoothing its creases with the edge of my hand. The bag matched the yellow paper coffee cup next to the sink.

Brina was still under the covers, eyes closed, but I needed answers. Now. I didn't shout, but I raised my voice to cut through the clouds of sleep. "Did you bring anything from Tortoni's yesterday?"

After it was out, I realized this wasn't the ideal morning greeting. By a long shot. Fortunately, she knew my bloodhound mode. She sat up in bed, scrubbing her eyes. "No. Just those two sandwiches from the Emerald Garden. They're still in the fridge, right?"

Her hair bobbed in bushy pineapple formation as she reeled my white dress shirt from under the bed and wrapped it around her. Someday, maybe soon, I'd suggest she leave a proper robe here. But I liked seeing her untidy this way, so different from her usual bohemian bling. This Brina, fuzzy and disorderly, belonged to me in a way the meticulous investigator never would. She approached the kitchen peninsula like a queen draped in graceful swaths of fabric. Lovely, golden, imposing, ravishing. I wanted to tell her all that, to convey something of the lyrical feelings filling me then. I should have, but the words wouldn't come.

Instead the blunt sandwich question stepped on the greeting I'd wanted to offer. "Did you bring Whip anything more than those subs?"

Without rolling her eyes, Brina laughed in gentle correction. "Well, good morning to you, too."

Despite the reproach, I was relieved by her laugh. Warmth spread through me, rising like a fireball from belly to ears, making my scalp tingle. The sun, burning through its early morning haze, ignited her eyes and licked flame across her cheeks. This was beauty, but nobility too; the closest I'd ever come to splendor in this life. Disappointed romantic or not, I liked the look of her in my shirt, the grace of her in my room.

When she spooned ground coffee into the filter basket, I liked her even more. She had her priorities in good order. She poked the machine to brew before she began tossing questions in my direction. "You think Whip got somebody to bring him lunch from Tortoni's? Who'd do that?"

"Somebody who knew he liked Tortoni's flatbread sandwiches." I reached two mugs from an upper cabinet and set them on the counter. "A good friend, maybe."

I'd visited the coffee shop a few times. The old-style café featured hand-crafted Italian desserts and cured ham cut paper-thin and piled high on homemade rolls. Its dark Italian roast coffee was neighborhood famous. Tortoni's founder had opened the shop in Harlem when he got off the boat one hundred and ten years ago. Sentimental inertia kept his grandchildren clinging to their family perch even as the neighborhood changed around them. Tortoni's was a treat, but it was twelve blocks from my apartment, too far for a casual drop-in. I only went there on special occasions. Or when I could hitch a ride.

"Or somebody who was too lazy to go any farther than the shop next door." Applying my own point of view to a situation often helped me understand the other guy. Especially if that other guy was sluggish, unimaginative, or cash shy.

"You're thinking Whip's pal lives near the café?"

"It's worth a shot. I figure Link is one of the few people Whip might call who'd actually come to the rescue."

Brina curled her fingers around a mug to considered this: "Carrying takeout from Tortoni's. Wow. And they say chivalry is dead." Mouth curved, nose crinkling, the tone fresh and light. Had she read my mind, divined what I'd wanted to say about her? Or maybe the first sip of coffee put that sparkle in her eyes. She could have awakened groggy or sorry. Ready to call it quits or take a formal break. But I caught a break instead. My clumsy greeting this morning hadn't soured Brina on romance. Or on me.

She drew close and dropped a kiss on my cheek. Eyes narrowing in mock horror, she dragged a nail through the stubble, then tapped my bottom lip. "If you want a lift to Tortoni's, Mister Detective, this train's leaving in fifteen minutes."

I scrubbed at my chin. "I'll be ready in twelve." Our conversation of the night before wasn't over. Questions lingered; feelings remained raw. But we were headed in the right direction. I straightened my spine, flexing the muscles along my shoulders as the gears of the day ahead slotted into place. Fortune, romance, lethal cash, wayward kids. For my plan to work, everything had to break right.

CHAPTER
EIGHTEEN

The goldenrod paint splashed across the walls of Tortoni's Café matched the yellow of its cups, napkins, menus, and takeout sacks.

Despite the sunny décor, the restaurant's interior was cool, which suited me fine. Five tables along one wall offered a roost and the glass-fronted counter promised fresh pastries. Another cup of coffee required something sweet to stop the sloshing in my empty stomach, so I ordered a slice of olive oil cake with a serving of fresh fruit on the side. The cake, plus a tall Italian roast, would put me in good with the crone crouching on a stool behind the cash register. I took the tiny table nearest the old lady and made a great show of savoring the cake. Which wasn't hard to do. It was light but earthy, a citrus icing sprinkled with shreds of lemon zest decorating the top. It felt decadent, eating this rich dessert before lunch, but I was in pursuit of vital information, so I told myself it was justified.

When I'd finished half the slice, I turned to the cashier and started talking. "That's hands down the best olive oil cake I've ever had."

She smiled and fingered the neckband of her yellow t-shirt. A large image of a strawberry decorated the front, which didn't do any favors for her figure, but I wasn't a fashion editor.

"You like that? My mother's recipe. From the old country."

"She sure taught you to cook *good*, Mrs. Tortoni! Your mother was an angel, no doubt about it."

Laying it on thick was my professional expertise. But when the old lady tugged at the elastic waistband of her black leggings, I knew I was home free.

"Yes, she was. One of God's true angels." She cast her eyes toward heaven and her freckled hand traced the shape of a cross.

After a moment of silence to honor her mother, I jumped on the train. "You know, speaking of mothers, mine sent me on an errand this morning. She's looking to find my sister's kid. Skinny and tall, about five-seven. You seen anyone like that around here?"

"Cute girl? A little darker than you? Yeah, I seen her. She came in here last night, visiting with Link, who lives upstairs. Maybe she's still around. I didn't see neither of them two come through here yet."

I dodged the argument over pronouns. "Yeah, Whip's a late sleeper. Probably still sacked out. You say they're upstairs?"

Her face clouded, red rushing to her ears. She ran a hand over tendrils hanging off the bun at the top of her head, fastening a few strands back in place with long black hair pins.

"Link's quiet, pays rent on time. But he's running with a bad crowd. I don't like to talk behind nobody's back, but I seen them with their eyes all red and their mouths loose like they's on drugs. Strung out, high. Whatever you want to call it. That's what they was. That Link, he's a bad 'un. Nasty piece of work. You ought to get your niece outta here pronto. I hope she ain't mixed up with Link and them others."

"I pray not, Mrs. Tortoni. That's why my mother sent me out looking. I got orders. And you can bet I'm not about to disobey my mother."

"No, you don't never want to do that. Never. Let me get Jimmy to run upstairs, check on your niece. What'd you say your name was?"

"You can call me Rook."

At that, she let out a shriek to startle her angel mother in heaven. "Jimmy! Get in here!" A pale child with feathery black hair and a miniature Yankees jersey scooted into the café from the kitchen in the back. "Jimmy, run upstairs and tell that new girl her uncle Rook's come to fetch her."

I hoped Whip would decide that, although I was a fake uncle, my concern for his safety was real. As I waited, I worked at the coffee, taking large gulps now that it was tepid. I wanted to save the rest of the olive oil cake for Whip, if he came.

———————

"Hey, *Uncle* Rook. Nice to see you again. How you doing, *Uncle* Rook?"

In the laying-it-on-thick department, Whip was no slouch herself. She'd changed from the clothes she'd worn two days ago. Now she wore slim-cut navy blue trousers with stingy cuffs rolled over bare ankles and a long-sleeved t-shirt featuring a globe hacked into pieces. The slogan "There is no Planet B" was blazed at an angle across the exploded world. Black high-top sneakers completed the statement. These new clothes told me she kept outfits at Link's place, an arrangement that alarmed me. This further sign of Whip's involvement with the hood set my teeth on edge, making it easy for me to play the fake uncle role with gusto.

When she approached my table, I wanted to hug her, and not just for the sake of the charade we were putting on for Mrs. Tortoni. But Whip extended a hand, so we shook instead. Man to man. I was glad to see him again; the worry washing through my veins since last night caused the café lights to flicker a few times. I passed a napkin across my eyes to wipe away the sweat. And maybe a few tears.

Whip lugged a bulging green backpack. The same one she'd carried to the hand-off with Kehinde that I'd broken up. She slung it under the table as she sat down, landing the load on my big toe. Not the bum foot, so I didn't mind. Too much. I wanted to talk, get our plan for the meeting with Martin Colón squared away. But with Mrs. Tortoni beaming at us from behind the cash register, I couldn't say much.

"Your Grandma Sabrina's been worried sick about you, Whip. You shouldn't have disappeared on her like that yesterday."

"Tell her I'm sorry about that. I really am. I was just antsy being cooped up all day, so when Link called, I took the chance to stretch my legs a little. I figured you'd see the coffee cup and the bag in the trash. At least, I *hoped* you'd see them."

Mist drifted across her eyes then, maybe a trick of the overheads, maybe a flash of the emotions she was holding inside.

"Kid, I'm not near as dumb as I seem." I pushed the plate over to her, a reward for the clues she'd left and reassurance that we were still on good terms, despite the runaway stunt.

"Not *nearly*. *Uncle* Rook."

As she finished off the dessert, I grabbed the empty coffee cup. Its shiny yellow exterior matched the warm golden color of the walls of the café. "Where's Link now?"

"Upstairs, still sleeping. He had a long wrestle with a bottle of tequila last night."

I studied the cup some more. On one side, bold black cursive letters spelled out the name *"Tortoni's"* with scrolls embellishing the *T*s and the final *S*. Under the name was the address of the café and the phrase, *"Buon Appetito!"* below it.

An idea prickled in my mind as I ran my fingers around the rim of the coffee cup. I could leave clues just the way Whip had. And hope Martin Colón was sharp enough to pick up on them.

With a napkin, I wiped out the inside of the cup, pressing the paper into the crevice circling the bottom to absorb the last drops of liquid. When it was clean and dry, I placed the cup inside the backpack, on top of the wads of twenty-dollar bills. I was careful to draw the zipper so the cup was not crushed, but nestled against the stolen money. This was the way out; I was sure of it. If everything fell into place, if every signal was received, if every hint was heard, I could save Whip.

At the high cost of betrayal, but a rescue all the same.

CHAPTER
NINETEEN

On second view, I guess my apartment didn't seem like a prison after all.

When we returned Whip dashed around me and into the room, flinging her backpack on the bed like before. But this time the grin broadcast comfort; if not exactly home, she was, at least, on familiar ground again. To honor Whip's new comfort, I tried to make the pronouns fit the way she wanted. He instead of she; him in place of her. But the words still muddled in my mind, letters and ideas blending into a slurry of awkward phrases. *His instead of hers. She, when Whip deserved he.* I kept my lip buttoned around the pronouns, but my thoughts still slipped and stumbled. I'd never get it right.

In the taxi ride to my place, I'd outlined the plan for our interview with Martin Colón. To paint the grim picture, I dropped somber terms like "violent threat" and "mob boss." I spiked my sentences with "silence," "ruin," and "kill." But Whip was excited for the conference. She was eager to meet the mastermind behind the giant money scheme she'd worked from distant street corners. She said she wanted to see Colón face to face, to hand over the cash she had taken.

Whip intended to apologize for her missteps and explain her charitable impulses. "He'll understand. Colón gets the big picture. It's how he operates."

"Don't be so sure, kid."

From her bubbling voice to her dancing eyes, Whip was moon-struck with what she imagined was the glamour of the meeting. Whip knew it was rare that a foot soldier got an audience with the head of such a vast organization. She was jazzed for the opportunity. I didn't tell her I'd already had the pleasure of meeting Colón and didn't look forward to a return date.

"This man is a prince. Royalty for real. It's like getting a chance to meet Jay-Z or LeBron. Up close and in person." Whip wrinkled her nose, then drew a long hand over her hair. I was an unhip clod, out of touch and hopelessly ignorant. If she was scared, she didn't show it. "This is my once-in-a-lifetime shot, Rook. I need to look sharp for this meeting. You gotta hook me up."

Looking her best for the appointment included a fresh haircut, it seemed, something I could help out with. "How do you know I cut hair?"

Whip shrugged, her conviction I was dim-witted growing by the minute. "You left me alone in here all day, what'd you think I was going to do? Sit in that armchair for hours and stare out the window? I snooped around, of course. Not much to see. How you live so *empty* like this, man?"

I looked around the place: one room, small, but not tight. Spare, but not exactly empty. There was the round oak table I'd picked up from the thrift shop, the cushions on the upholstered armchair were plump, even if their yellow stripes were a bit garish. A peninsula holding a TV separated the living room from the galley kitchen. If you sat on the bed, you couldn't see if dishes were piled in the sink. Next to the bed was a tall chest-of-drawers. I'd given Brina the bottom drawer to store a few items of clothing to make sleep-overs easier. Herb the cat loved to perch on top of this dresser next to a pile of paperbacks, watching me while I slept, pouncing to wake me in the morning. My newest purchase was a wool rug that stretched from the bed, under the table, almost to the two stools at the peninsula. I liked its swirls of deep blue, gray, and camel flecked with yellow. The effect was warm and soft. Cozy was a word I never used. But I thought it fit the rug pretty well.

Whip asked how I could live in an empty place like this. Good question. For which I had no ready answer. Caught, I pulled my shirt tails out of my belt for air conditioning and plopped in the chair.

Whip continued pacing from the bed to the kitchen and back, like a lion cub straining at a leash. "Two boxing magazines, a TV, and three books about some Navajo Indian detective in New Mexico. There's nothing to *do* here, Rook. How can you stand it?"

Tony Hillerman's novels caught the dry, spare mood of the West pretty well. But Whip was looking for something more than crime fiction. "I did come across all that fine barber equipment in the bottom drawer in the bathroom. You got some high-grade tools. You a pro or something?"

"Used to be. A long time ago. I fixed up a few heads during my stint in the army. And after, when I landed here in Harlem, I put those tools to good use."

"Well, dust 'em off and put 'em to good use on me. I need a shape up before I meet the prince of Harlem."

Our barber shop was makeshift, but we did a good job on the fly.

I shoved aside the two toothbrushes to make room on the bathroom counter for a folded towel. On it I set clippers, electric razor, trimming shears, fine-tooth combs, hair brushes, straight-edge blades, and a bone-handled whisk. While I laid a moat of towels on the floor, Whip dragged a bar stool from the kitchen peninsula and placed it in front of the mirror.

Establishing my professionalism and seniority was important. "I do the cutting. You do the sweeping after. Got it?"

"Deal. Just don't get the line crooked. Got it?"

"Never have, kid, never will."

We negotiated for several minutes over how high above her ears the skin fade would start. The width of Whip's three fingers equaled two of mine, so the debate raged until we settled on using the corner of her eyebrow as the marker for the design. The fade would be low and dignified, more junior exec and less skater-boi.

Whip wanted to keep the jagged twists at the crown, but I persuaded her that a moderate trim off the top would suit her face and style. I shot down Whip's request that I slice a design into the right side of her head: I refused to carve the lightning bolt logo from her backpack into the haircut. This was a formal business meeting, not a gangbanger convention.

I didn't have a regulation barber's cape, so I grabbed a spare pillowcase for Whip's shoulders. To save the t-shirt from getting soiled, she pulled it off and flung it over the door of the shower. Underneath, she'd wrapped a broad band around her torso. The white bandages extended from her armpits to her navel, drawn tight like a mummy's swath around her narrow brown body.

The question popped from my mouth half-formed: "You wear that all the time?" Stupid, invasive, raw, but real.

"Yeah, this year. I have to."

"You didn't last year?"

"No, but now, I do." Whip hunched shoulders until the skin pulled tight, exposing the knobs in her spine. Her gaze dropped toward a shadow near the door sill. "This year it changed."

My curiosity had hurt. "Sorry. Not my business. Forget it."

She shrugged and hitched the bandage higher. "It's cool. I got it worked out." For some time, I'd wondered how Whip concealed the budding breasts, how she made this body conform to her male self-image and identity. "I got some good lessons. And it's all cool now."

Seeing the care she took to convert her figure into its proper shape forced tears to the corners of my eyes. She didn't duck or cringe. She didn't ask me to look away from the exposure. This was who he was and the honesty invited me to accept him in full. The honesty of these open gestures humbled me. If I could, I'd earn this honor. I wrapped the pillowcase across his back and knotted it tight at his throat. This superhero cape fit him.

Unlike many barbers, I worked in silence. I didn't have gossip to share, and I didn't crave idle chatter. So, once the design elements had been settled, we fell into a comfortable quiet.

We were too silent for Herb. The nosy cat sauntered in to inspect our salon. He stretched on the floor beyond the door jamb to supervise my hushed performance. Jaw clenched, Whip studied my movements, eyes flicking across the mirror's reflection of my hands and face as I circled. I bent low to shape up the line crossing the nape.

Whip broke the silence. "You think I look like a boy?" The question slipped from her narrow frame like a bird's murmur; if I hadn't crouched so close, I might have missed the words.

I stared into the mirror. I could tell the truth. Sure, the truth would bite. Whip wanted to be an adult; maturity meant dealing with truth and its penalties. I'd be helping Whip take a necessary step toward adulthood. Truth would be just a small sting, a bee's momentary jab. The honor I'd gain would be a rush. I was a straightforward guy. Honest. Plain. My rule was respect direct questions with direct answers. Shading the truth was lying, right?

I remembered Whip treating me to apple pie. Jabbing an elbow into the belly of the goon, Kehinde. Sobbing over Zaire's death. Teasing about Brina. Sneaking away, then leaving yellow-splashed clues for me. Sharing the intimacy of the chest bandage. We'd been through a lot in a brief time. Was my honesty worth the harm to Whip? This truth would inflict a grave injury, open a gaping wound no one could repair. Whip trusted me, valued my sincerity. Believed I was an honest man.

So, I'd lie. It was the right thing to do.

Peering into the mirror, I pinned Whip's eyes with my own. "Yes, you look like a boy."

"For real?"

"Yeah, for real." The lie slid off my tongue with ease. Fiction cut the muddle, acceptance burning the rubbish of secrets and pretense I'd clung to. I inhaled, a shuddery breath so deep, the cat swiveled his ears in my direction. The lie freed me to see the kid as he was, whole and uncompromised. A boy who deserved a chance to grow into the man he wanted to be. When I exhaled, the gust blew tiny clippings from Whip's neck. I resumed work on his hairline, the shaver vibrating against his skin.

Affirmed, Whip talked. "I been this way long as I can remember. The first time I knew, I was five. It was in Sunday School at our church. The teacher told us to line up for roles in the Christmas pageant. One line for shepherd boys, another line for milkmaids. I was a boy and shepherds looked like more fun. So, I got in line with the boys. I stood there until the teacher snatched me by the wrist and dragged me to the milkmaid line. She said, 'You get with the other little girls.' Then she found my mother. My mom spanked me right there in front of the other kids. Yelling that I'd shamed her. Then, to make sure I understood, she beat me again when we got home."

Whip's eyes were dry as he unearthed this old story. Mine weren't. The buzz of the shaver shook my hand.

"Link isn't my boyfriend, you know. Just a friend." My heart spun cartwheels as Whip raised a question I hadn't asked. The shaver hummed a low soundtrack for this tender moment. I lifted it from his neck, so my trembling wouldn't wreck the precision of the line.

He continued. "I like girls that way. Not boys. I mean, I don't have a girlfriend or anything. Maybe someday. That's what I'd like. That's what got my mom so angry last spring. When I told her that, she just went *off*. Blew up. That's why I ran."

"And that's when you found Eddie?" Fitting the pieces together was simple.

"Yeah. He showed me how to wrap this band around my chest. 'Not too tight/Never at night,' That was his rhyme. He taught me lots. How to deal on the street. How to defend."

"Eddie?" I moved in front of Whip to speak face to face.

"Yeah, sure." The upturned lip registered good-natured scorn. "You do know he's trans, right?"

I closed my eyes against the comical reflection of my jaw hanging slack below the gaping hole of my mouth. "I never guessed."

Whip laughed, a loud blast flaring through the narrow space. "And you supposed to be a detective!"

The gleeful shout startled Herb from his sprawl in the doorway. The scorn in Whip's taunt translated into the cat's disdainful yellow glare. A slide show flashed through my mind: Eddie's slight frame, short stature, high tenor voice, hairless cheeks. Not looking, I'd missed the clues.

I shrugged and lowered my gaze, the corners of my mouth curling as hoots bounced over the tiles. I administered a few short swipes to the kid's neck with the whisk, brushing off the clippings and curls. "Good thing I'm a talented barber. Or you'd be out of luck."

Whip expanded on the pauper's story. "Eddie said he was Edith back in the day. Said trouble trailed him: a wrecked marriage to some super-violent dude. Didn't have no kids to make them stick together. Then hospital, lost job, and the street. His life broke apart in a big crack up. He told me not to follow him as an example. Said I shouldn't end up like him. With bums for neighbors and a mattress for a home."

"He's right, you know." I stroked a washcloth over Whip's nape. "About the homeless part anyway."

"I know."

"You've got greater chances ahead of you, Whip."

He twisted on the stool, admiring his handsome reflection. He ran long fingers over the neatly cropped line at the brow, then snapped a smart salute. "Don't worry, I got this. I'm going to make my chances into something big. Something smart. You'll see."

––––––––––––––

Our stop at the Friends In Deed settlement house was meant to be a drive-by, not a visit.

"I need a real shirt, a button-down, instead of this wack t-shirt. I need to up my game for this meeting with Boss Man Colón tonight."

I told Whip he looked fine. But wearing my usual black slacks and black shirt, my style cred was in serious doubt. We took a cab from my apartment and instructed the driver to wait at the curb. Whip intended to make this call as brief as possible.

But he was greeted as returning royalty when he galloped through the doors of the dormitory on the way to his mother's second floor room. Joyous clamor from other residents brought Keisha Reynolds running from her office in the main building of the compound.

"Whit, we've been so worried about you! Worried sick. Let me take a good look at you." She made that examination hard to do by crushing the boy to her bosom, thumping slaps across his back. With her bursting heart on her sleeve, sheer gladness pumped through the dingy corridor.

"I'm alright, Miss Keisha. I've been doing alright for myself."

"I can see that. You look good. You really do. You've filled out. Grown up too." Keisha lifted her head from Whip's shoulder, shooting a grateful glance my way. Tears streaked her cheeks and dampened the boy's collar.

I nodded, but kept my mouth shut. This wasn't my show. Not yet, anyway. I hung back from the reunion, leaning against the corridor wall, watching Whip's face for signs of distress. I was ready to step in if he indicated the contact was overwhelming. But the smooth contours of his forehead and easy creases around his eyes said he was comfortable for the moment.

"Miss Keisha, I can't stay long. I need to get a shirt. I got an important business appointment tonight, and I don't want to be late. Is my mom around?"

"Let me call her. She's in a computer class, but I know she'll bust out of there when she hears you're back. You stay here and let me fetch her."

When Keisha hustled away on her mission, I dropped into a threadbare chair in the lounge. I parked Whip's cash-stuffed backpack at my feet. From that distance, I could keep an eye on Whip in the corridor without intruding unless he called me. Leola Covington's shrieks hit even before she burst through the door into the building. Though these yelps were glad, the decibel level was identical to the one she'd used when howling in grief over the cell phone images of her lost child a few days ago.

Leola had one mode for dealing with the world: full-throated holler. "Oh my God! Oh my God! Whitney, is it you? Are you come back?"

"It's me, Mom. It's me."

I expected a fight, but Whip didn't rage against the use of the discarded name. Whether moved by a new-found maturity or just hoping to gentle the meeting, he let his mother's embrace boost them into a dance of joy. She swung him off the ground, then held him at arm's length, then gathered him to her breast again, stroking the shorn sides of his head with her rough fingers.

Old name or new, girl or boy, this was her baby and that's what mattered.

Propelled on a flurry of kisses, Whip and his mother departed for her room. Keisha Reynolds invited me to her office for celebratory coffee. Our next meal might not come for hours; the homemade ginger cookies she pulled from a corner cabinet looked extra tasty. Her face glowing with the heat of her conviction, she rattled on, praising me for finding Whip and bringing him back, chattering about what a blessed day this was and how a way always opens in the universe when we just let ourselves follow divinity's sacred leadings.

I smiled as if agreeing with her warm-hearted beliefs. But this day was far from over. And night's harvest was sure to be dangerous, even cursed. Keisha's assurances reinforced my silence, not my confidence. Nothing good could come from the meeting with Martin Colón. Scarfing this cheerful woman's cookies and coffee, I swallowed guilt along with the calories. I was carrying an innocent boy to a possible appointment with death.

Keisha's coffee heated a new idea. Whip's reunion gave me time to steal away for a return visit to Tortoni's Café. He wouldn't miss me. Thirty minutes max: ten-minute taxi ride there, ten minutes back. And ten minutes for a sociable chat with the hoodlum, Link Ruiz.

CHAPTER
TWENTY

My favorite geriatric barista welcomed me for a second round at Tortoni's. When she beamed this time, the chipped front tooth flashed between liver-red lips. "Nobody stays away long from Tortoni's. One taste of my olive oil cake, and you're hooked for life. Right, Mr. Rook?"

The yellow walls of the little restaurant cast a sickly glow over the cash register as I leaned over the counter. I dished my best grin and pulled out my wallet. "You are so right, Mrs. Tortoni! Can you wrap two slices to go? Thick as you can make 'em." The wink sealed the deal. Cheesy but effective.

As she hoisted herself off the bar stool, I threw a casual footnote: "I'll pick up the package on my way out. I'm running upstairs for a quick chat with Link. He's around, isn't he?"

"Yeah, go on up. He ain't come down yet. Probably still in bed, the lousy creep."

The apartment door was unlatched, so I invited myself in. Link absent, I toured the space. His one room was half the size of mine, which soothed my ego. Single bed, rumpled brown paisley sheets. The short couch fussed with flowered pillows and a tatty orange blanket must be where Whip bunked. A large brown suitcase bulged under the bed; with no chest of drawers, this would be where Link kept his clothes. I bent, unfastened the suitcase, and poked through his meager wardrobe until I found what I was looking for: the switchblade was nestled next to a pistol inside a brown track suit. It was a snub-nosed .22, ugly and lightweight. I pocketed the gun along with the knife. Two folding chairs covered in brown pleather completed the furnishings. They flanked a low table whose stained surface was the final resting place for a dead tequila bottle.

Out of respect, I set the bottle on its feet. At that moment, Link walked in. His nose and eyelashes dripped water. The dab of toothpaste at the corner of his wispy moustache said he'd completed his daily wash-up in a bathroom down the hall. Unprotected by the red bandanna, the razorblade and hearts tattoo on his neck twitched like a stoned hooker. He'd seen me at the Palace and in Lonnie's Diner, so he knew who I was. But that knowledge didn't make him happy to host me.

"What the hell you doing here? Get the fuck out!" Link hiked dingy beige sweatpants higher on his waist. A drop of water wandered over smooth brown skin from ribs to belly button.

"Or what? You going to call the police?" I sat on one of the folding chairs and pointed at the bed. "Sit down, Link. I've only got a few minutes and a few questions."

"I don't take orders from you, motherfucker." A clear declaration, yet he flopped on the bed as requested. "What did you do with Whip?"

"I ask the questions, kid. Not you." He glowered but said nothing, so I continued. "What's your connection to the Colón mob? Tell me and I'll clear out."

"And then you hobble to the cops flapping your lips? Nah, I'm not talking to you, gimp."

"I'm not police and you know it. In fact, the opposite. I'm meeting the big boss tonight. Maybe I'll put in a good word for you with Martin Colón. Polish your resumé. You'd like that, wouldn't you?"

Link thought for twenty seconds, visions of gangster sugarplums dancing in his head. Ambition beat anxiety as a sneer tilted his lips. "Okay, crip. What you want to know?"

I had him. "The signals with the flower pot. Was that Whip's idea? Or yours?"

His eyes bugged at my inside knowledge, but his voice stayed cool. "Mine, of course. Whip couldn't invent something complicated like that. That little freak couldn't think her way out of a two-foot ditch."

His disdain for Whip rubbed raw, but I wasn't fighting that battle now. Threats would shut Link down. Flattery would prime him to spill more. "Yeah, I figured. Too intricate. You and Kehinde are the brains behind the cashing operation, right?"

"Yeah, sure. Me and Kehinde run it. The kids in the crew follow my lead."

Not a chance. Bragging slathered over lying was an idiot's combo. But I could use the advantage to get the details I needed. "And that shooting in the park. That your idea or Kehinde's? Or maybe it was his twin brother Taiwo who ordered it?"

"It was Kehinde pulled the marker on that kid. Actually, Kehinde said to take out Whip. Said she was skimming from the cash haul and needed to be punished."

"But you switched the order, didn't you, Link? You decided if you kept Whip alive you could blame future shortfall on him. Take as much money as you wanted and keep pointing the finger at Whip." Winging it through an explanation was dicey. But playing to Link's ego was my strongest bet. "So, you decided to miss Whip and shoot the other kid instead. Right?"

"Yeah, that's just what I did." Satisfaction stretched his weasel face.

"You pulled the trigger?"

"Sure. Taiwo drove the van, Kehinde rode shotgun. But it was me they handed the semi-automatic."

"You opened fire in a crowded playground. At night." The rising tone strangled my words.

But Link was too far lost in the romance of his story to notice my agitation. "Sure. What you think? My eyesight is twenty-twenty, fool. I see plenty good enough. Even in the dark. I done this before, shot dudes at long distance. I'm that good. Top-grade marksman. I saw Whip talking to the little brother." Link screwed shut his left eye, extended his arm, and aimed a finger at the wall behind me. "I leaned out the rear window and *plow-blam-blam*! Off he goes! Like that, see? Simple."

Taiwo, Kehinde, Link. The trio had executed my friend Zaire Martin without a thought. Simple. The boy didn't matter to them. Only to Whip and me. I'd gained the intel I needed. The churning gut and strafed heart came extra. "Yes, I see."

Link dragged a hand over his mouth, chipping off the crusted toothpaste. "So, you gonna pow-wow with old man Colón tonight? For real?"

"Yes, for real."

"That's dope!" Link's black button eyes glittered. Under the narrow ribcage, his lungs pumped double-time. "I wish I could be there, though."

"Sure, Link. You'd be a hit with the big guy." Sarcasm was wasted on this asshole, but the bite felt good anyway.

A wrinkle dented his brow. The thug leaned over, reaching for the suitcase and his hidden knife and gun. Maybe he had second thoughts about spilling so much inside info to an unreliable stranger. Or maybe he just wanted his binkie pacifier.

Before he could discover the loss, I stood and patted my pocket. "Don't worry. I'll take good care of your little friend, Link."

"Hey, you can't steal that! It's mine!" The inside of his mouth flashed pink above fine tendrils of beard.

"So what? You going to call the police?" This was where I came in. Time to exit before our chummy chat curdled. "Gotta run, great shooting the bull with you, Link." At the door, I touched the scar behind my ear, then thumbed the rusty latch. "You should lock this thing, you know. Safety first."

In the taxi, heading to retrieve Whip from the settlement house, I wrapped a yellow napkin around Link's greasy gun. I slipped it and his knife inside the bright yellow Tortoni's sack. Whip and I could enjoy the two extra thick slices of Tortoni's olive oil cake before our meeting with Martin Colón.

CHAPTER
TWENTY-ONE

Kehinde's beat-down started with taps to my solar plexus. Two stiff punches. Not much more than sledge hammers tickling my gut. Then he got vicious. He owed me a pounding after I'd smashed in his face. And for inciting the execution of his brother, Taiwo.

Twilight cast violet shadows over the street, so the casual brutality of our encounter was shielded from view. Even so, I was glad Whip was blindfolded before the blows began. I didn't want him to see what happened. My hands were zip-tied behind my back. I was thankful they decided not to bind the boy as well. The thug landed four solid knocks to the kidneys, two on each side for symmetry. Pain flared from a rib. Cracked or bruised, the ache swelled with each breath. Then he spun me around to deliver four more blows to the stomach. I grunted, but swallowed the moans. No need to alarm Whip or give Kehinde any satisfaction. Gasping, I braced for a knee to the groin, but none came. Small favors.

The brute pinched my chin between dirt-caked fingers. "Boss said to bring you to him in one piece. He didn't say nothing about the condition of the piece." Sparing my face and balls was just smart business practice.

Laughing with gusto, he showed large teeth in maroon gums. Then he turned toward Whip and grabbed his belt. Kehinde patted the kid's stomach gingerly, then with greater force. Whip sniffled and leaned away. I lunged toward Kehinde, but two goons clamped my arms. As his hands moved over the band around Whip's torso, Kehinde's eyes bulged.

The ugly face wiped clean as a first-day-of-school blackboard. His eyes narrowed to slits, then he stuck the tip of his tongue into the humid air. He'd reached some conclusion that clotted in his mouth. But he wasn't sharing, not out loud. He turned his foghorn voice on me. "Relax, man. I'm not gonna mess with your girl. *Whatever* she is. I'm just doing my due diligence. The boss would rip my throat if this little punk smuggled a piece or a phone into headquarters."

Kehinde unloaded two more low punches into my gut; a bubble of bile clogged my mouth. A cry seeped across my tongue and I gargled that too. Deep panting disguised the moan. The goons wrapped a black blindfold over my eyes. It didn't block the lightning flashes behind my lids. Then they shoved us into a panel truck with cheery advice: "You and your lollipop lean back, relax, and enjoy the ride."

We bounced on the vehicle's corrugated floor as it rumbled through rush hour traffic. The van smelled of wood shavings and turpentine, maybe a handyman's truck stolen for the event. Something sticky pressed against my cheek; maybe blood. I hoped it wasn't paint, I didn't want the nice green shirt Whip had picked for this party to get soiled.

"You okay?" Whip's voice was small, whispering to avoid antagonizing the two guards watching us.

"Yeah, okay." My mouth tasted like last year's well water: sulfur laced with lemon peels. The jolting of the van drove pain through each breath; but Whip sounded good, that was something.

When we stopped, dank air and the slap of water against wood indicated a dock, not Colón's lair. The transfer was fast, down a wooden ramp and then a short flight of unsteady steps. We'd been dropped on a barge of some kind; the vessel's gentle rock was nothing like the violent propulsion of a motor boat. We were on a river, not heading for open water; street traffic rumbled nearby, a mechanical tide contracting and expanding as we floated along.

Whip breathed easily beside me, knee pressed against mine, shoulder bumping my chest in time to the jostling of the barge. Steady blowing in and out, no rush, no panic; though engaged and excited, the kid was calm in this strange situation. His presence soothed me, as if he cast some sort of eerie magic over the moment. I timed my breathing to his, hoping the mind game would dull the shooting pain in my gut and the ache in my tense heart.

Without sight, the other senses expanded. Water lapped at the sides of the barge, wafting briny odors over us. The tang of fish and barnacles, the mildew of old ropes, their moldy smell undercut with rust and decay. Circling overhead, seagulls squawked, their cries farther away or closer as the warm air currents lifted them. A sharp toot-toot from a passing boat interrupted the drone of the barge's sluggish engine. The vessel's rough wake sent tremors through our own. With my hands still cuffed behind me, I struggled to regain my balance on the deck bench. Would we ever reach Colón's den?

Time swept us forward in little jolts, rocking us like swells under a simple log raft. It was still early evening. Without the sun's warmth, I had no clues about the direction of this river voyage. Our captors were silent, but near, always watching. We tipped and swayed, rolling with the tide.

Despite the uncertainty, the enforced blindness, and our captors, Whip seemed calm. Finally, I asked Whip in wonder: "You're not afraid, are you?" Was he braver than me? Would our whole bond be framed by that question?

"No, I'm not." He sounded small but sure as his voice murmured through me.

"Why? What makes you so positive?"

"Well, he asked for the meeting. And I'm bringing him back his money. So, he's got no reason to kill me now, right?"

This next warning would be unwelcome, but I had to deliver it. "Money isn't the only thing that motivates him." I meant revenge, intimidation, control. The grisly currency of the gang world.

But the kid took it the other way around, finding solace in the idea that Martin Colón might be prompted by some noble urge beyond crass greed. "Then that's lucky for me, I guess."

Was Whip chuckling? Not a snicker or a rude hoot, a low gurgle. A sweet and uncorrupted giggle. Laughter for a river cruise on our raft, a lazy summer jaunt with a picnic lunch at the end of the ride. Drifting wishes would cradle us for a while. But the ride had to end. And the spoils from this cruel picnic could only be bitter.

———————

Kehinde jerked the blindfold from my eyes as we rushed through rain drops to the glass doors of a sleek office tower.

The bare marble of the lobby gave no clues to our location; no signboard named the building tenants, no gilt letters declared who owned the high-rise or what purpose it served. I craned my head to look for address numbers above the entrance. All I saw were the first showers of a looming storm.

When our armed escort reached the brass-framed elevator bank, it divided in two groups. Kehinde and another man hustled Whip past the sliding elevator doors and disappeared. I yelped, but three men slammed me through a heavy utility door.

In the dark stairwell, one clown offered a cheerful explanation through snaggled teeth: "Kehinde said you liked to walk. So, we're taking you up the old-fashioned way."

When I cut my eyes at him, he clapped me on the back. "Don't worry, bruh. It's only fifteen stories. We'll make it by sunrise."

CHAPTER
TWENTY-TWO

Wicked stitches in my stomach drummed in time with the droning pulse in my three-toed foot.

One good thing about this chorus of pain: the hurt stopped me from gasping like an idiot as I entered the grand reception room when we arrived at the penthouse. My jaw dropped, but I didn't have breath for anything more eloquent. Stupid was my only play, so I clung to it.

Martin Colón had decorated his loft like an ice palace. Emerging from the gloom of the stairwell, the bright glare of the space reduced me to the blinking fool he'd hoped I'd be.

Down the middle of the giant room stretched a bare table of ashen wood. Under it was a pale Oriental rug with an intricate border pattern in lavender, moss, and cream. The carpet was so big the Plexiglas chairs around the table could be pushed back and their feet would remain within the rug's boundaries. Confusing smells flowed around the room: a combination of lime and peroxide with a whiff of baby powder drifting over the top.

Colón sat at one end of the table on a throne of white leather and steel, the light of a crystal chandelier glinting off his bald head and glasses. The pillowy white of the loft made his black moustache and eyes pop in contrast. Beyond the conference room were glass coffee tables and bleached leather couches outlined against tall picture windows. The summer storm had exploded in furious display, distant lightning bolts lurching across the purple sky over a grove of Jersey high-rises. Against the backdrop of rain-streaked windows and columns of clouds, Colón's head and shoulders loomed powerful, like he'd conquered this kingdom of storm and light along with the city below it.

Colón's informal dress—straw-colored slacks, open neck white shirt, no tie—was casual enough to disappoint the star-struck Whip. Glamour came in many forms, on a scale from Kanye to Denzel. The prince of Harlem played at the subdued end of the spectrum. He was cool and dignified, the knife-sharp creases of his pants signaling the deluxe intensity of his style.

Recessed canisters in the ceiling showered the table with icy glare, the parallel rows of lamps exaggerating the length of the room. Colón's lieutenants and assorted muscle lined the walls, black men and Latinos, with a sprinkle of Asian toughs. The whole United Nations, minus Europe, had shown for the party. The men's slouches clashed with the formality of the setting. These casual stances said the boss owned their souls, but he couldn't dictate their postures. Over hunched shoulders, abstract pastels in aluminum frames beamed with fake cheer.

In the hushed ranks, I spotted Kehinde near the head of the table. A bright spotlight emphasized his resemblance to his late twin Taiwo: same harsh sneer, same darting eyes. Next to him was a woman with Colón's tawny coloring and dark hair, his blunt features carved into feminine beauty on her face. I'd met Liana Solis when I played bouncer at her child's birthday party eight months ago. Later I'd learned Colón's daughter was the mob's money man, a treasurer with golden fingers and a heart of flint. This princess was lethal: I knew two men whose executions she'd personally ordered. How many more men—fools or rivals—had been strangled in the purse strings Liana held so tightly? As I moved toward the table, her black eyes cut a narrow trace over my body. Neutral interest sparked her features, but no overt recognition. Like I was a new silk suit she'd ordered online, but now considered returning. Was Liana protecting me? Or herself? I kept a straight face under the examination, eyes on the carpet. No need to provoke her father without intent.

Bookend to Colón's daughter, another woman, the deadly muse Crystal, leaned against the opposite wall. Her sweet scent was a reminder of that grisly night we'd met in the Bronx Swamp. She was the source of the baby powder floating through the room now. Encased in a black leather vest and tight pants, Crystal smirked at me, her hazel eyes chilly and focused. Then she winked as if we were old comrades. Her abrupt execution of Taiwo sealed a bond between me and the pint-sized assassin. Creepy, but still a connection. I bounced my eyebrows in acknowledgement, no need to insult her. But I kept my mouth straight, in case Colón didn't approve of flirting with the hired help. No use fouling the deal before we'd reached our chairs.

Walking between the parallel lines of silent foot soldiers, I spotted Whip, already seated to the left of the gang boss. Colón tilted his head at an empty place next to the kid. I slid the chair out, in no hurry to sit down. My foot, back, and stomach begged for relief. But in this fix, careful silence was my only resource.

As I sat, I whispered to Whip. "Stay quiet; I'll do the talking. Got it?" He nodded, but from my angle I couldn't catch his eye to be sure he understood.

Colón was in a sociable mood, as if we were gathered at his table for an after-church Sunday supper. "It's good to see you again, Rook. I hope you had time to think about your options since our last meeting."

Were we old chums now? Reunited after weeks of separation instead of combatants who'd met a few hours ago in mortal struggle? I clamped my teeth tight to make the skin shiver over the muscles in my jaw.

"And my dear friend Norment Ross and his charming daughter? Sabrina, isn't it? How are they?" What did Colón know about my involvement with Brina? How far did his spy network reach? I kept quiet, not trusting my voice to stay cool.

"Please give Sabrina my fond regards when you see her next." Colón's attempt to claim her, to leverage her against me grated. Peeling the slimy smile from the gangster's face was tempting. Idiotic but enticing. Instead, I straightened my shoulders, then my neck. The immediate stakes were higher than this vague threat to Brina. I'd grapple with that snake another day. Bantering wouldn't cut it; small talk implied we'd already settled every issue between us. But we were far from that conclusion.

Seated now, wind returned to my lungs, I reached next to Whip's knee and hoisted the green backpack onto the table. I pushed it toward Colón with enough force that it almost toppled over the edge. "Here's what you want, Colón. It's all there. Count it, if you wish."

The line sounded good; maybe it was even true. I didn't know if Link might have lifted some cash the night before. But this exchange was all about bluffing, and I was going to ride that fake claim as hard and long as I could. I gambled the mobster wouldn't count the money until we'd left the table.

Colón unzipped the bag and pulled out the yellow Tortoni's coffee cup, his brow furrowing. He set the cup to one side and piled the blocks of cash into a little square fort in front of him. When he spoke again, it was to the kid. "You call yourself Whip, right?"

"Yes, sir." A proper altar boy chirp for the scene.

"Now Whip, you may wonder why I am so concerned about what we all would agree is a minor sum of money." Colón ruffled the edge of one stack with his thumb, lips thinning at the sound the bills made in the stale moonlight of the loft. "In an operation that moves millions every transaction, why would I even note or care about the few thousand dollars you skimmed in your little charity escapade?" Colón relaxed in his chair, pausing to peer into Whip's face. "Can you guess what it is?"

The boy had the good sense to look down. "No, sir."

"The reason is as plain as an old fairy tale: If I let you get away with this theft, then others–less generous than you–will imagine they can get away with it too." Colón removed his glasses, then adjusted them higher on his nose. Was his eyesight failing? Or was this a theatrical gesture, a pause before the main speech?

The mobster and I started when Whip broke the silence. "But I can repay the money, Mr. Colón. Every penny of it. I will."

"I am sure you would repay me, Whip. Your honesty is hit or miss, but your sincerity is deep. I have no doubt about that at all." Colón looked around the room at his assembled henchmen. With an audience present, the dramatic impulses of the man were impossible to stifle. I stiffened, ready for the bragging to launch.

"Young man, let me explain my operation in a few phrases that even you will understand. This organization gets its strength from a simple principle: although the scope is broad, each of the individual cells operates independently. By design, one doesn't know about another." Colón sighed and steepled his stubby fingers together in front of his chest. "I suppose I sound like an old-fashioned Bond villain in a movie, gloating about some wicked plan for global domination."

His head swiveled as he studied Whip and me. "But the fact is I have harnessed the brainpower of hackers around the world. At my command, they have infiltrated the systems of credit-card processing companies in India and in Nebraska. They have breached banks in the United Arab Emirates and Singapore and Tokyo."

He spread his hands in a wide arc as he concluded with a flourish. "I have tapped the dynamics of the Internet and the limitless possibilities of cyberspace to create an elegant network that is bold, fast, and so new its potential has only barely been mined. *This* is the big picture."

Blinking rapidly, Colón shook his head as if returning to earth. He fixed his serpent gaze on the kid again. "Whip, you see my operation is a complex one. But I maintain its machinery with a single all-important lubricant: confidence. I have to have confidence in those who work for me..." Here he paused and looked directly at the men and women lined against the wall to his left. "...At all levels down to the lowliest cashing crew. And just as important, every part of the operation, even the most humble, must have confidence in my word." Colón raised his voice to a rich tenor peal. "And they must have confidence in my ability to exterminate anyone who crosses me."

The warning wasn't shouted, but the walls vibrated with its power even so.

"It's not the money, it's the message. You get me?" Colón turned his bulging eyes on Whip, red threads flashing in the rancid cream around his dark pupils. "That is the confidence your little pilfering threatens to undermine, young man. So, a lesson must be taught. An example made for all to see."

Whip quivered next to me, finally understanding the danger of this situation. His hands trembled until he pulled them from the table and clasped them in his lap.

The negotiation–that's exactly what this was–now turned to me. "He's too young, too weak, Colón. And you know it." I murmured to emphasize the intimacy of the exchange. "You hurt the kid; you diminish yourself. You kill him; you prove just how small you are."

I paused, stretching for the type of dramatic touch that seemed to snare Colón's attention. His eyes bore into mine as I continued. "If this operation is as big as you say it is, then you don't want anyone getting the idea you're just another two-bit racketeer, do you?"

To signal he was listening, Colón cocked his head to one side.

I shifted my eyes toward the yellow paper cup on the table between us. The mob boss followed my intense stare and grimaced until the skin shimmied below his full lips. Colón picked up the cup, inspecting it closely, and then reached under the table. From his pants pocket he pulled out a simple switchblade, the kind of weapon a lonely boy just starting in life would carry to give himself a little courage.

I continued my argument now that I knew my opponent's attention was focused where I wanted it to be. I shot my boldest arrow and prayed it hit bull's eye: "Let him go. He means nothing to you, Colón. Killing a kid like this signals your weakness, not your strength."

Colón fingered the knife's button release, and it sprang like a sinister tongue in his hand. "Rook, you make a good point. My generosity can reach even farther than the bloody grasp of punishment."

He lay the cup on its side, carefully sawing around the bottom, while making sure not to nick the high polish of the table's surface. When the circle was complete, Colón removed the disk and set it down flat.

I plunged on, knowing my message had been received. "I'll guarantee Whip leaves the city by tomorrow night. And he stays gone. You have my word."

Colón nodded once, a predator's cool jerk. And then with a swift thrust, he sliced the cup down its seam from top to bottom. He pressed the stiff coated paper on the table, smoothing it until the convex surface flattened completely.

"I accept your pledge, Rook. And give you my own: no harm will come to this boy during the next twenty-four hours. But if he's found in the city after midnight tomorrow, he will be eliminated."

Running his hand over the script that spelled out Tortoni's Café, Colón stopped his index finger over the black lettering of the address. He tapped the address twice as if to memorize it. He'd received my message.

Our filthy bargain made. "Do what you have to do, Colón." The exchange of one life for another was fixed. "But leave this kid alone."

"I'll do what needs to be done. Count on it."

I sighed, a whoosh of air I regretted as soon as it left my lungs. Dropping guard while still at the table was a rookie error.

Colón chuckled and pressed his flabby chest against the hard edge of the table. "But I require a little more to sweeten our deal. To make it worth my while. I'm sure you remember my offer, Rook." A buffed fingernail stroked the knife blade to underline his message. "I want you in my organization."

Bitterness gathered in sour gobs at the back of my throat, blocking speech even if I'd known what to say.

"You're reluctant, I can see that. But you're in debt to me now. You owe me, Rook." He stretched in his chair, a gentle smile hovering on his lips. "I will demand repayment when and where I wish. That's our bargain. Take the deal and this kid lives. Turn me down and, well…"

Colón's eyebrows raised to form a question he already knew the answer to. He had a roomful of witnesses, but a nod from me wasn't enough. I had to speak out loud to seal the contract.

The word knocked around my throat for a second or two until I coughed it up: "Done."

I couldn't look Whip in the face right then, maybe I never would again. But from the corner of my eye, I caught a frown playing across his wide brow. The kid was worried for me, afraid of the filthy swamp I'd stepped into. He got this part of the contract, knew I'd sacrificed something precious. But he didn't recognize the other half of the deadly deal I'd made to save his life. If I had the power, Whip would never know.

I puffed out a sour breath. Our interview with the prince was over.

———————————

Without even a farewell salute from Colón, rough hands hustled me and Whip toward the exit.

As before, two men pushed Whip into the elevator, while Kehinde and a pair of his pals escorted me to the stairs. The walk down wasn't so bad: my battered insides had unknotted enough to stifle the pain and my foot was only screeching at a dull roar.

No one spoke on the descent, just a grunt or two. I kept my guards moving at a quick clip. When I reached the sixth-floor landing, I slowed as if the pace was killing me. War wounds are a torment, but they have their uses. As distractions or ploys, old injuries serve instead of fading away. I dawdled for two more floors, reducing my speed and exaggerating my limp with every step.

"What's the matter with you? Why you dragging?" Kehinde was close behind, his angry breath lacing my neck. "Step on it, Rook."

I picked up the pace. I skipped steps from the fourth to the third floor. At the top of the next flight, I stopped. I pressed my left shoulder against the wall. My right foot flew to the side. Kehinde's momentum carried him across the landing. My outstretched ankle clipped his shin as he passed me. He plunged over the edge of the stair, tumbling head first into the darkness. A simple trick, but the crash was dramatic. Legs in the air, Kehinde slammed into the concrete block wall. The thud was dense, like a 190-pound potato sack hitting dirt. Thick and compact, no bounce. I clamped my mouth over the laugh. Zaire's death wasn't paid in full, not yet. But this was a solid down payment.

At the bottom of the stairs, I stepped over the crumpled body. Kehinde's head was twisted at an odd angle, but he was still breathing. Heavy, wet huffs shuddered from his chest. Creamy bubbles dotted his lower lip. A white bone shard jutted through a rip in his sleeve like a ship's broken mast. Maybe there was blood on the black shirt, maybe not. My armed escort halted on the step above, their hot breath on my ears.

I wasn't sure how my two travelling buddies viewed things, so I asked straight up: "You think he looks alright?"

I couldn't see their shrugs in the dark, but their answers were as clear as sunlight on the Jersey shore, "Nah."

In solidarity, I hiked my shoulders. "Me neither."

After three seconds, the goons hopped over their fallen chief. No pause, no worries. We descended to the lobby in silence. Whip and the other guards were waiting at the revolving door. The kid looked relieved to see me; the jerks didn't ask about their missing leader. Out of sight, out of hoodlum minds. Thug loyalty was flexible, easily purchased, quickly transferred. Kehinde wasn't around to give orders. Maybe I'd aced the initiation ritual. The crew considered me a member of the Colón tribe now. For whatever reason, they skipped the blindfolds and plastic ties for our return trip to Harlem.

At one-thirty in the morning, Whip and I rolled from the van at a corner four blocks from my apartment. We walked the rest of the way in the warm rain. Whip didn't ask any of the questions I'd feared might pepper our passage. He didn't talk at all. Maybe exhaustion gagged him. Or maybe, grateful to be free of Colón's den, he dropped the cheery patter. Whatever the reason, I was glad for it and let the silence sweep us home.

We could profit from the quiet of this night while it lasted. The bruises and deceit of the next day would stun us soon enough.

CHAPTER
TWENTY-THREE

Even at three minutes past twelve the next night, the Port Authority terminal buzzed with running humanity.

The building surged with people on the move: fleeing, dodging, skipping, escaping. Whip and I elbowed our way from the ticket counter. Pushing through the crowd to find the berth for the westbound bus took linebacker nerves and the tenacity of a nun. Excitement mixed with humid nausea in the rush. Contending emotions fouled the air with a blend of piss and vomit. The grime on the tiles, the lilac smog of cigarette fumes rising two stories above our heads, the fatty stench of pastrami, and the ripe odor of candy-flavored perfume all told the same story: getting out was the right move.

As I handed Whip into the twelve-fifteen bus, I slipped an envelope of cash into the kangaroo pocket of his black sweatshirt. "This should last you until Chicago."

Three hundred dollars from a jar in my kitchen cabinet plus another eight hundred Brina and Norment kept in the safe in our office. I'd square the loan with them later. The money wasn't much, a paltry sum to start a new life. But it was all I could corral in a pinch. And one thousand one hundred dollars was four hundred more than I'd had in my pocket when I arrived in Harlem. The kid had optimism, health, and eagerness in his favor too. He'd do alright.

Whip hoisted the navy-blue backpack over his shoulder; I'd bought him a new knapsack to start his new life. Inside it, he'd crammed all his earthly possessions: a pair of jeans, three t-shirts, four pairs of boxers, the lucky green button-down shirt, and a hair pick. Sneakers and a maroon sweater completed the stash. I assured him he could find other essentials at his destination; even the dull Midwest had shopping malls.

He patted the thick envelope and laughed. "Far past that, I bet."

"Chicago's far enough." I followed Whip down the bus's narrow aisle, the backpack butting against my stomach each time he paused.

When he reached an empty row, he looked up with a startled expression. "You going with me?"

I shook my head. "I can't. You know that."

He knew my obligations–to Brina, to Norment, to Martin Colón–kept me in New York. I pulled him close, my hands tight around his back. With his head on my chest and his eyes hidden, talk came easier. I whispered into the kinks of his baby-soft hair. "You need to forget everything. Harlem, Link, Colón, me. Everything. Understand?"

I hugged him until he squeaked. Then I tugged the hood around his ears so I could bring his face close to mine. Tumbling into the brown depths of his eyes, I struggled to get my words straight before I spoke them. "That's the best thing you can do, Whip. If you keep remembering, you'll throw away any chance for fun or purpose or connection in your life."

"And my mom?" He posed the simple question without emphasis, though it carried a world of meaning. I hadn't let him speak with Leola before we left for the bus station. He would tell her too much if he saw her again. Like ripping the Band-Aid from a raw cut, this break from New York had to be brisk and clean. And final.

"I'll look after her. And Eddie and Odette too. I got them under my wing."

Whip leaned back to look me in the eye. His gaze zig-zagged across my face as thoughts churned and bubbled. Confident of the immediate safety of his old connections, he settled on another set of worries. New city, new situation, strange contacts. If his mind wasn't boggling, he'd be the most cold-blooded kid on the planet. Whip could tackle these fears if he expressed them, so I raised my eyebrows to encourage him.

"But I don't know any of these Chicago people." No whine or whimper. This was a tough kid.

"They're good people. You'll see."

"That Smoke Burris. You said he's a detective too? Like you?"

"Yes. He used to work here in Harlem, with Brina and her dad. Now he's in Chicago with his own outfit."

"The Comet Detective Agency?"

"That's right. Comet. I gave you the address. It's in the Bronzeville neighborhood. Near South Side. Smoke knows you're coming. I'll text him again, remind him to meet you at the bus station."

"What do they do at Comet?"

If I could spark Whip's curiosity, his fears would soften. "Security, investigations. Solving big and little cases around the neighborhood like we do. You'll find out the details for yourself."

"This Smoke. He a friend of yours?"

"More a colleague." It was the bare truth, but my hesitation sent doubt wriggling through the kid's mind. I'd never met Burris; Brina had suggested the Chicago connection, and Norment had made the arrangements with his former employee. I trusted their judgment and I wanted Whip to have confidence in mine. I squeezed both scrawny arms to make my point. "I believe in him, Whip. That's what you need to know. I trust Smoke Burris with your life. You should too."

Whip lowered his head, forcing me to bend to hear his next words. "Does he…Does he know about… You know… about me?" No tears, but the teeth worrying his lower lip forced water to my eyes.

"Yes, I told him. I told him enough. I said you were a good kid. The best. *That's* what he knows about you." I lifted his chin until his eyes met mine. "I accept you for who you are, Whip. And he will too."

The bus grew hot, clamping on me like a serrated trap. My head hurt, my side ached, my heart galloped. Regret bludgeoned me and I choked on the next words. "Do what I say, kid. Forget me. Forget us all. Forget New York. You'll be fine."

Whip made no promises. A slight smile stole across his mouth before he kissed my cheek. He hoisted the backpack into the overhead rack and took his seat, releasing me to flee into the night.

One day later, an hour after dawn, Archie Lin called me to a crime scene near the docks. He pointed at a black body bag stretched on the damp planks. Mossy stains spread across the wood slats around the lumpy sack.

"Brina said you'd want to see this." The high sun had forced Archie to loosen the knot in his red-and-gray checked tie. "You know this mope or something? Harbor police pulled him outta the river this morning."

It was early, but already a stripe of sweat blemished his white shirt. His left hand fiddled with the belt buckle where it chafed against his belly. Rank insisted he keep the dark gray suit jacket even in the heat and he suffered for his status. Too bad for him. Maybe if he made lieutenant, he could ditch the stiff clothes.

I'd been expecting a call from Archie, told Brina to be on the lookout. But even cushioned by anticipation, the blow landed hard. Standing beside Archie, sickness swamped me. I bent at the waist, jamming my fists into flexed knees. No matter what they say, psychic pain hurts as much as the other kind.

Cops in short-sleeved uniforms strolled with their thumbs hooked into their belts. Techs peered through thick eye glasses, plucking shreds of evidence the way lovers pick daisies. A photographer captured the scene for official files, a dead cigarette dangling from her lip. Nobody cared who was inside the body bag, whose life had been snuffed or for what dirty cause. Against the white sun, seagulls wheeled overhead. Pigeons strutted at the edge of the crowd, hoping for a handout. The air smelled dank and discarded, like soiled bed sheets.

Archie unzipped the body bag and folded one of its lapels so I could get a good look at the head.

A damp bush of black curls crowned a thin dark face whose faint moustache and wispy beard were plastered to his cheeks. Black eyes, flat as buttons, stared at nothing. The jaunty red bandanna was knotted twice around Link's neck as if to protect him from the murky waters of the Hudson. Its cheery color mocked the blood crusted inside two bullet wounds at his right temple. Under the bandanna, the dull blue hearts and razorblades tattoo sagged on his gray skin. I stopped cataloging details. If I noted any more, the memories would sicken me forever. I'd told Whip to move on and forget. Now I needed to swallow the same medicine.

I was silent so long Archie repeated the question. "Some kinda local gangbanger, I figure. You know him?"

"Yes." I looked at my sneakers, then nudged mold from a wooden slat near the body bag.

After another long pause, Archie pushed on, official exasperation giving way to friendly concern as he softened his voice. He stepped closer, cocking his head to catch my eye. "So? Who is he?"

I stopped twitching my feet and stood at attention. Guilt for this death surged through my veins. I'd killed Link as sure as if I'd raided Tortoni's Café and pulled the trigger myself. But I didn't regret the bargain I'd struck with Martin Colón. I'd made a choice, traded Link's life for Whip's.

The deal was right. Whip was safe from harm. Launched on a new life in a new city with people who'd protect him. The flurry of text messages Whip had sent from Chicago was a balm on my flayed soul. I'd studied the photos he'd attached: the white t-shirt with the deconstructed globe was familiar, as was the sly grin. The sight of the husky detective Smoke Burris standing behind Whip, a paw clamped on the boy's narrow shoulder made me laugh. My decision was painful, but right. Unsentimental and tough, Burris matched his city. He was the mentor a kid needed. Whip was in good hands and I could rest easy. I'd done my job, the best I knew how. I'd sacrificed Link's life, my own honor too. But the deal was good.

My friend needed an answer, so I gave one. "His name was José Abraham Lincoln Ruiz. Called Link. Worked a cash crew for the Colón mob. He was twenty years old."

Archie squinted as a sunbeam caught him in the eye. A dozen questions galloped across his open face, six about this dead thug, six about me. Being a smart cop and a smarter friend, Archie posed a question that tackled both halves at once. "How do you know him, Rook?"

I pried open my jaw to give him something. "He's connected to that drive-by shooting in the playground. And to the kid Whip. I'll fill you in later. Not now, Archie. But sometime."

Archie frowned, waiting. If I stopped there, I sounded forlorn, wounded. Like I'd given up, tossed the case in a trashcan, abandoned my job. The way Colón's hoods had ditched Link's body.

That wasn't me, not the real me reflected in Archie's wondering eyes. So, I gave him something. A slice of truth so small and thin it was almost transparent. But the something was true. Something real, a hard clue fitting Link's murder into the bigger picture. Something to show Archie I could be who he believed I was.

I reached into my back pocket and drew three white index cards. The night I'd seen Link push the red geraniums to send his coded message, I'd written the license plate numbers of each passing car next to a brief description on these lined cards. Nine vehicles in all.

I shoved the cards into Archie's fist. "Link's cash crew drove these cars. Some of them might be stolen. Some could be in a Jersey chop shop. Or half way to Mexico by now. But if you check, you might find one or two still in the city."

Archie unfolded the first index card, scanned it, then slipped all three into his breast pocket. He patted his heart, where they lay. "Thanks for the lead. This'll help."

"Sure." Nothing more to say, nothing that mattered.

Archie tossed the official phrases. "You'll have to give a formal statement. Dates, times, names. The works. Tomorrow's soon enough. This goon's not getting any deader."

I'd hand over Link's switchblade and gun tomorrow. Still wrapped in the yellow napkin from Tortoni's, they might help the cops piece together the jagged bits of Link's short, foul life. I turned to end the exchange with Archie. The only good thing about having a bum foot is the permanent limp covers all sorts of pain. Makes it hard for friends to tell if you're suffering from the same old complaint or something new. Something you don't want to talk about.

I tried to escape, but Archie caught me before I'd taken three steps. "Say, pal. You around tonight?"

"Yes."

"I'll drop by your place. Maybe bring a six-pack. Modelo or Genesee okay with you?"

"Yeah, sure. You pick. See you later."

Archie caught me, but that was alright.

CHAPTER
TWENTY-FOUR

Done polishing off the six-pack of Modelos, Archie left my apartment at midnight. Brina arrived twenty minutes later. Like they were a tag team, wrestling my unruly emotions into submission. Archie had exhausted my conversation, polite or otherwise. So, only a few sentences littered the next two hours. I didn't want to talk and neither did Brina.

After, we lay side by side in bed; drifting clouds covered the half-moon hanging low over the rooftops outside the window. Hazy light turned the sheet a blurred purple in the valleys around our legs. With my index finger I traced the path of a drop of sweat along the silvered knob of Brina's shoulder. It skittered down the incline toward her throat, paused, then disappeared into a little shimmering pool between her breasts. I drew her to me. I longed to be complete in her once more. But this nostalgia of the body was a dangerous sentiment: vague and bitter-sweet emotions replacing hard calculation. Keeping your head in the here and now was vital to doing your job. To staying alive. Pining was for fools. This sensation felt like homesickness, joy and sadness mixing together in equal measure.

I sat up and shrugged to repel the sentiment. She padded to the kitchen, bushy hair jumbled on her bare shoulders. Her departure blew a draft across my neck. The chill sent a shower of goose bumps falling to my waist. I shrugged again to recapture the lost warmth.

She returned from the refrigerator with a plastic bottle. "Plain tap water okay?" Bouncy with fake lightness: "I could spike it, if you want."

"No, I'm good. Thanks."

We pulled the sheet around our hips and passed the icy bottle for two silent rounds. Then she tilted and her words vibrated against my ribs. "Most people–regular parents–take two decades to do it."

"Do what?"

"Get a child. Raise him. Love him. Lose him. Miss him."

"Yeah. Regular parents."

Her cool lips moved against my collarbone. "But you, you made the whole cycle in ten days."

"Yeah, two kids. Zaire and Whip."

I couldn't see her face. The darkness deepened in the room. She took a gulp of water to soften the words. "Is it enough? Do you think you'll miss it?"

"Miss what?" Her intent was clear, but I let her voice the fear.

"Miss having children. Raising kids." Her damp syllables tripped into a gasp.

"Yeah, I'll miss it." Direct question, direct answer: the truth 'til it hurts. "I wanted it. For a long time. But I never thought it could happen for me. Maybe growing up without a father, I just figured I wasn't cut out to be one."

"But you are, you know. Parent material, I mean."

"Think so?"

"Yes, I do. You've got brains and the toughness it takes to be a parent. And a big heart packed with loyalty and kindness."

I gulped. "Maybe, Brina. Maybe." To squelch the sob welling in my throat, I retreated to a quip. "But I doubt I'm your ideal man. Far from it."

She caught my shift in mood and pressed her smiling mouth against mine. "Of course not. That would be Idris Elba." She hummed a throaty chuckle. "You know, for my thirtieth birthday, I wished for Idris Elba. Didn't seem like too much to ask. Not in the grand scheme of things.

But instead of delivering Idris, my friends baked me a triple-decker chocolate layer cake."

"Sure: tall, dark, and delicious. The Idris Elba of desserts."

"Exactly!" Warm laughter bubbled from her body to mine, consoling me.

With the breathing room and confidence she'd given me, I turned the conversation again. "And what about you? Do you want children?"

"Yes, I want them. I don't know if it'll happen for me. I'm not great mother material, either, growing up without a mother." She huffed a short laugh at our mirrored histories. "But yeah, I do want kids."

"And if it doesn't happen, Brina? Kids might not be in the cards for us, you know."

"Yeah, I know."

I sighed with her, then gathered a stronger voice to bring home my thought: "But now I realize, *this* is enough. The life I lead now. This life *we* share now. *This* fills me up. And I'm alright with that."

"You are?"

"Yes, I am. Now." Not seeing her face, only feeling her warm breath against the tears on my cheek, made it easier for the words to tumble out.

"I wasn't before Whip. But now, after him, I'm okay. Whip is enough."

———————

The next days tiptoed by. With every phone call, every rap on the office door, the cement block of anxiety tied at my ankle wobbled but didn't plunge.

Two days after Whip left, I visited Eddie and Odette at the Palace for a round of show tunes and nutty stories. They studied the photos of Whip in Chicago with sagging mouths and bulging eyes. As if I'd rubbed a magic lantern and shown them an exotic land reached only by flying carpet.

When Odette scampered to the far end of the vast hall in search of a hospitable booze bottle or pizza slice, Eddie transformed his worry into his companion's. "Odette's sick about all this, Rook. Fretting something awful."

"Tell her she doesn't need to worry." I scrubbed a hand over my mouth.

"I told her, but she won't let it go. You know how she is. Hangs onto people and things. Even when they're shreds and scraps. She hangs on."

"Yes, I know how she is."

The old man pulled a folded piece of slick paper from under his mattress and thrust it at me. "I ever show you this?"

It was a glossy pamphlet from the Ballard Hotel, a fancy mid-town pile I'd never go near. The decades-old cover was creased at upper and lower corners. Below the hotel's name was a full-color photo of a gorgeous woman in a strapless silver dress. Her black hair was wound into a crown, the head thrown back in rapture. Eyes closed, red lips parted over strong teeth, her brown shoulders gleaming under a gauzy spotlight. One hand raised a microphone to her open mouth, the other hand caressed the sleek surface of a piano curving around her lush hips. Commanding, even in a faded picture, Odette's beauty provoked passion. Falling for her was easy. I didn't resist.

Eddie smirked at my swoon. "She doesn't know I found it. Dug it from her grocery cart one day when she was off searching. Back then, she was called Odette Bard."

"I thought she was a fashion model." It was my turn to goggle and gape.

"No, no. She made that up. Invention, fakery, and fairy tales. Or just forgetfulness. Odette was a cabaret singer. Played all the top hotels and clubs back in the day."

I whispered to mark the revelation. "She's stunning, Eddie."

"Sure is." He sighed, breath ruffling dust from the slick folder. "She sure is."

I opened the brochure, taking care with the brittle paper. The program boasted of Odette Bard's four-week engagement at the Campion Room of the Ballard Hotel. Promoters were excited, reservations were required, top-drawer pleasure was guaranteed. Under the headline, "Bard at the Ballard," quotes from gushing music critics were tossed like confetti. The hotel bragged Odette would be accompanied by the renowned Joe Thurman Jazz Trio. A small photo showed Thurman at the piano, his handsome grin as broad and white as the keyboard.

"*This* is Thurman?" Mouth hanging open made my words bobble.

"Yep. Her piano man. I thought you'd want to know."

I studied the little photo again. Bold lantern jaw, fawn-yellow skin, high domed forehead under black hair. Even in the faded image, Thurman's light eyes flashed with magnetic allure. The smooth smile on the musician's lips belied the tension curling his fingers. Confidence like that revved the engines of most women. Possibilities jumped through my mind. "You think he was more than her piano man?"

"Don't know. Don't dare ask." Eddie raised his shoulders, then dropped them to continue the speculation. "I used to think Thurman had to be her husband or boyfriend. Father, brother. Or even a baby. 'Thurman, Thurman, Thurman.' All the time 'Thurman.' Had to be somebody important. Somebody lost and gone."

The old man tilted his head. "Then I found this and solved the mystery. I can see where he favors you some; I get how Odette made that connection. Now I'm a detective, just like you!"

I nodded and placed the fragile program on the bed between us. Eddie plucked it with yellowed fingernails, then closed his eyes. He held it to his nose, savoring the fragrance of his companion's glamorous past. He slid the pamphlet under the mattress, then scooted closer to me, settling his weight on this precious clue.

I leaned until my shoulder touched Eddie's. Prescribing forgetfulness was my sole trick, so I did it again. "Whoever Thurman was, best forget him. He's lost now."

"You got that right. Lost and gone now. Except in her mind. Odette don't never forget. She don't take good to losing people that's close to her."

"Nobody does, Eddie."

"That's what got her so riled up about Whip going away like this. Another one lost and gone." Eddie speared me with his sharpest look. All the years dropped from his face as his bark-brown eyes took my measure. "Think he'll make a go of it there in Chicago?"

"He'll do alright. You taught him well." Raised him right and loved him well, I should have added.

The old man smiled, pink tongue showing in the ragged gaps between his teeth. "Did he say so? Whip said that for real?"

Eddie pushed two fingers into the metallic tangle of hair above his brow. He dragged a palm across his furrowed face, wiping away tears without shame.

I squeezed his damp hand in both of mine. "Yes, he said so, Eddie. And I say so too. You taught him well."

————————————

Whip's mother wasn't so easily consoled.

Leola Covington cried, ranted, and cursed me for stealing her baby girl. But a new job in a grocery store and an apartment Keisha Reynolds helped her find filled the empty hours. I promised Leola when danger had passed, I'd send for Whip. I said I'd arrange a visit so she could start on the path of reconciliation with her son. She flinched at my words, acceptance still a long way down the road.

It took forty minutes of coaxing, but I finally convinced Keisha and her boss Sondra Crane that the mysterious money they'd stored in the shoebox all these months really did belong to Friends In Deed. I learned later that they used Whip's donation to replace the heating and air conditioning system in the dormitory wing for women and children.

In the immediate aftermath of Whip's departure, the Ross Agency tackled a few new cases, little problems with simple solutions. I passed dreary hours in my office phoning delinquent clients in search of payment, using a tepid script Brina prepared. Link's death weighed on me; my heart wasn't in the work, and as I drifted through these doldrums, Brina cut me some slack.

But the stay was temporary. As she often said, we were a detective agency, not a *defective* agency. How long before the boss's patience ran out?

CHAPTER
TWENTY-FIVE

Not long. All I got after Whip's escape was three days breather.

As distraction, or penance for unnamed sins, on Thursday Brina demanded I type the world's dullest expense report. I didn't want to go home, couldn't sleep anyway. Ten-fifteen at night seemed like a good time to start. I doused the overhead, preferring the narrow cone of light from the desk lamp. I was banging on the report, when our landlady Mei Young materialized from the depths of the purple shadows in front of my desk.

The scarlet slash of her lipstick made her message harsher than the plain words she spoke. "You got a man looking for you downstairs, Rook. Come right now." Mei's black eyes blared worry. But she seemed excited too, like a kid skipping third period gym to watch an X-rated movie. Judging by Mei's jitters, whoever this man was, adult content and illicit danger surrounded him.

When I didn't jump from my chair, she raised her voice. "I said *come*, Rook! You heard me?" Mei Young was used to giving orders: she governed the motley brigade of kitchen help in her restaurant with a firm hand. None of the cooks, busboys, waiters, or dishwashers spoke Mandarin, but they all complied without a hitch. Mei doled advice, instruction, and verbal spankings to everyone as needed, no back talk allowed.

I didn't wait for the snap of Mei's third order. "Hold your chop sticks, I'm going."

The Emerald Garden was closed for the night, its kitchen dark when I entered the rear door. I felt my way through the familiar stain-less-steel terrain without faltering. Mei had cut the lights in the front of the restaurant, but left a single overhead lamp shining on a table at the back of the room.

Theatrical lighting suited Martin Colón well.

He was alone, slumped, his back pressed against the wall. The corn-silk-yellow shirt threw a glow on his face. His clasped hands lay on the Formica tabletop, rough and brown like folded burlap. If he owned any piety, I'd swear he was praying.

"Thank you for joining me, Rook."

Like I had a choice.

When he raised his chin, I dropped into the chair opposite him, no greeting, no salute. This was professional, not social. Mei hadn't even left a glass of water for the mob prince to suck while he waited for her to deliver his summons.

"I'd say long time no see, Colón. But it hasn't been near long enough."

"All business, is it? No appetite for pleasantries, as usual. Rough edges unpolished by even the vaguest effort at civility. You must be a difficult man to live with, Rook."

"So I'm told."

"As you wish then." His teeth clamped tight, leaving a dark slot for the words to slide past. "I haven't forgotten our little bargain. I assume you haven't either?"

"I remember. I delivered my part of the deal: the kid is gone. You delivered your part: a two-bit thug is dead."

Colón straightened his shoulders at my defiant tone. "That's not the entire deal, as you well know."

"What do you want?"

"I need your services in a delicate matter. It requires discretion, diligence, and quite possibly bravery." His black eyes drifted to a spot high on the wall over my head.

"Vague isn't my game, Colón. What do you *want*?"

"Do you remember my driver, Crystal Figueroa? The young lady you met when we first visited a week ago in the Bronx Swamp?"

"The little dead-eye assassin? Yeah, I remember her."

Colón coughed, a delicate rumble at the back of his throat. We might have been discussing candidates for the PTA board. "I need you to drive Crystal to Tampa. Tonight."

"Why can't she drive herself? She's a pretty good wheelman. Good with a Glock too, I recall."

If my harsh characterization of Crystal bothered him, he didn't show it; his features stayed smooth and his voice low. "Crystal can't take on all that driving solo. She has other concerns."

"What do you mean 'other concerns?' You're talking like a crumbled fortune cookie."

Colón breathed an elaborate sigh through pursed lips. "Crystal has a baby to look after on this road trip."

"*Her* baby?" Stupid question, but the only one that jumped off my tongue.

"Hers." A beat for the dramatic effect he loved. "And mine."

I jerked against the red vinyl cover of the chair. Under my weight, the plastic split in protest. "Christ! You expect me to play bodyguard for your woman *and* your kid? Colón, you're high as a vulture. You been popping those pills your corner boys're pushing around town?"

The glitter in his eyes vanished with a snap. "I'm sober. And you'd better be too."

"I'm not going anywhere for you. Not until you give me the straight story."

"You don't have any room to maneuver, Rook." He coughed over my name, like it choked. "You can't issue demands."

"My chauffeur services come with a price. You talk. Or I walk." I stiff-armed the table like I meant it. The threat was a bluff, but I thought I had nothing to lose.

Colón hacked again, then shrugged. He wanted my help with this errand. It meant a lot to him. Learning this cold-blooded mobster was a hot-blooded lover pricked my interest, so I raised my eyebrows to get him started.

He took a deep breath to spew words across the table. "Not a long story, really. Crystal's folks moved here from Tampa the year her big sister was born. I came across the family in Spanish Harlem a few years later. Her papa worked corners for a crew I ran."

The sneer stained my voice. "And darling Crystal just stepped into the family business? Like an inheritance? Very old-world."

"It was a natural fit. My best lieutenant was Crystal's boss. Little fella, always sharp dressed. Named Roger Thorpe, but everybody called him 'Carnage,' because one time he killed eight gangbangers in a single raid. Tossed a collection house, saved my life too. After that they all called him 'Carnage' out of respect, because nobody wanted to go up against him ever again."

Colón's heavy moustache curved at the bloody memory, and he ran a hand over his naked scalp. He was on a roll, the gangland glamour of his life's arc glittering as he spoke.

"Carnage taught Crystal everything there was to know about the business. About reading people, figuring out their hearts, studying their eyes, learning their moves, getting so far inside their minds you know all their drama, all their dreams."

His head bobbed in rhythm with the recitation of the lessons of Carnage, the hoodlum folk hero.

"Knowing when they're lying to save their own sorry asses or bull-shitting to hide a mistake somebody else made. Or getting ready to sell you out or screw you over. Fucking them before they fuck you. Carnage knew when to pull a smile. And when to pull the trigger."

I nodded, scorn tugging at my lips. "This Carnage sounds like a genius. He learned all those lessons at your knee?"

"He didn't gain these insights on his own, that's true." Sly modesty fit the mobster's command style. So, Colón's instruction was the source of Crystal's remarkable powers of intuition and the eerie clairvoyance I'd witnessed in our deadly meeting in the Swamp.

I leaned forward in the chair, eager for more. These insights into the internal dynamics of Colón's mob held my full attention. The information might help me someday. If I lived long enough. I threw a question to prime the flow of gangland gossip. "And Crystal was a good student, hunh? Got all *A*'s in Carnage's classroom?"

"Yeah, she did." Pride poured from him now, ripe and unfettered. He was delighted with his master creation, like Michelangelo gazing at the ceiling of the Sistine Chapel. "Crystal was the best I *ever* saw–pimps, hawkers, cutters, runners, lamp posters, dustmen, baggers, sweat skimmers–none of 'em better than her."

"She was your prize disciple. And naturally you fell for her."

"Yeah, I did."

"And lucky thing, she fell for you too."

"She did." He blinked three times, surprised at the turn of his fortunes. This was love, clean and simple as an unfired bullet. Pure, if that term could be applied to a mob ruler and his lethal muse. "I called her 'Baby Carnage.'" Colón gazed through the restaurant's picture window, raising his voice as his head shifted.

The declaration sent a shiver down my back. "Why?"

"I called her that after Carnage passed. Because when it happened, Crystal was the one I picked to step up, to take his place, work by my side in a position of trust."

I hesitated to interrupt, but I pressed on, pushing aside this veil of nostalgia and affection. "How did Crystal become your lieutenant?"

In the gloom, Colón's jowls seemed to recede and the bags under his eyes shrank to wallet-size. Maybe twenty years didn't drop from his face. Maybe it was a trick of the shadows and he didn't really grow younger, or smoother, or slimmer. But he looked vulnerable, the love-struck kid peeking from under the slick, hard surface.

"I'd heard some gossip about Carnage planning to pull off a side drug deal with some Russian skags, skim off a little profit on his own account. I couldn't let that kind of thing stand. Betrayal like that spreads through your whole organization. Like an infection rips through a body, until the fever brings you to a raving end."

He worried wrinkles on his knuckles as he pulled together the last chapter of his story. "Carnage was my best man. But he betrayed me. He had to go. Based on the information I had, I ordered the hit." Colón hesitated only a second, until the next affirmation carried him forward. "And I was right. I knew for a fact what Carnage had planned. Because I had the inside line from Crystal. *She* was the one who snitched on Carnage."

Another pause, but the end was a boulder rolling downhill now, dragging him on to the last. "And I told Crystal *she* was the one who had to pull the trigger."

"And she–she did it?" Stuttering made the question kink in my throat.

"She did. Put two bullets above Roger's ear while he dozed in the car beside her."

Hissing at this raw confession, I bit my lip to recapture silence. I wanted that water now. I pushed from the table to poke around in the dark kitchen. I found two glasses and filled them from the tap. Colón seemed grateful when I shoved the water across the table to him. He sipped, I gulped, until we each had drained half our portions.

My mouth still felt dry, the words scraping a crust from my tongue as I spoke. "But if Roger's dead, what's the danger to Crystal now?"

"We have other enemies in the city. Some from the past. But my concern is for the newest adversaries. They're the most treacherous. I think you know Kehinde Adebosin."

"Yeah. I heard he took quite a tumble." Pressing my lips down, I stifled the laugh. "His arm healed yet?"

"Still in a full-body cast." Amusement flitted across Colón's face.

With that to go on, I added to Kehinde's resumé. "His twin brother Taiwo was the one Crystal offed in the Bronx Swamp, right?"

"Yeah. Kehinde thinks I've put a target on his back too. So, he's put one on mine. In his view, your little attack on him was sanctioned by me. After that assault, I didn't avenge him by having you killed. This confirmed the assumption for him."

"So, Kehinde thinks I'm your man."

"Right." Colón shrugged as if bored by the obvious. But to make his reasoning clear, he continued. "Kehinde is ambitious. Out for revenge. He won't strike at me directly. Not yet. But if he can harm the people closest to me, then he'll make that his first priority."

I'd fallen so far down Colón's crazy sewer this gangster logic made perfect sense. "Your baby. A daughter or a son?"

"A little girl. JoJo. Yomaira Sonia. I named her after my grandmother. She's two years old now, chatters like a little monkey." Smiles fluttered across Colón's face, fond ones and proud ones chasing each other as his thoughts raced ahead of his words. "Pretty as a sunrise. Reads the whole alphabet, sings and counts in Spanish and in English too."

I hummed, a tiny buzz escaping my lips to urge Colón onward.

"If I can, I'll get her out of this life. Out of this war zone. My JoJo deserves a better shot than this." Colón was in love. With this assassin Crystal and their baby, with the glimpse of a redeemed life they represented.

Doubt waded into this crisis, making me raise the issue. If Colón wasn't thinking clearly, I had to. "But will Kehinde let her go?"

Colón snapped a fierce reply. "He doesn't have a say in it! He takes orders from me, I'm his jefe. My mission is his mission. But JoJo doesn't have a mission. I already have one daughter in this business. You know Liana. I lost her to the gang life a long time ago. But I don't want my little JoJo scouting some fucking street corner before she reaches eight. A lamp-poster in this army by the time she turns ten. I'm her father, and I can do better for JoJo than that." Colón gulped to suppress the sob surging in his throat.

Before caution stopped me, I touched the thick veins on his hand. "I can get JoJo out of the city for you, Martin. That's what you want, isn't it?"

"You get JoJo to my mother in Tampa, and they'll find a way to get her to the island. You do that and our deal is settled. You get my baby away from here safe. Then we're clear. I promise."

He pulled a phone from his pocket, poked at it, then turned the screen toward me. Photos flashing across the surface showed Crystal seated in the shotgun bucket of a white Prius. A black hood framed her snub-nosed profile as she stared through the windshield.

"They're at the corner. The tank is full. Get going now."

I shook my head. "I can't leave like that. I need…"

"You need *nothing*, Rook." Colón pulled a wad of cash from his breast pocket. He tightened a red rubber band around it and slipped a debit card under the elastic. The same rubber bands had wrapped the cash bricks Whip had stolen and donated to the settlement house.

"This should get you to Florida and back. Crystal has the PIN number. And her own money too."

"No." I lowered the next words to avoid whining. "Give me a day to plan. Then I'll do it."

"You do it *tonight*!" The gangster jumped from his seat. He leaned across the table and grabbed my shirt collar. Right-handed, he twisted the cloth into a noose under my chin, hoisting me an inch above the chair. I gagged as he swept a water glass onto the floor with his left hand. Roaring blood behind my ears screened the clatter and smash.

I seized the wrist at my throat and dug my thumbnail into the fragile gutter between his veins. His pulse fluttered then throbbed as pain surged toward his elbow. Colón released the chokehold and I sank into the chair. My gasping matched his, breath for humid breath, as we glared through the gloom.

Prodding the phone again, Colón scrolled to a new set of pictures. "Tonight. Understand?"

He shoved the cell to me. The shots were unfocused, but the subject was clear: Whip climbing the steps of a red brick bungalow; Whip sitting in a soul food restaurant window, Whip shadowed by the metal scaffolding of elevated train tracks. Colón's spy network had found the boy in Chicago. If I didn't comply, the kid would be in danger again. To save Whip, I had to make good on my promise to Colón.

I stroked the red-hot ring pulsing around my throat. "Give me the keys, Colón." I swallowed a sigh as he dropped the chain on top of the cash and pushed the pile at me. He knew where I lived, where Brina and Norment lived. Now he knew where to find Whip too.

"Good decision. You're a smart man, Rook. I always knew it." White teeth sparkled under his black moustache. "That's why I trust you with my baby. You'll keep her safe. I know it. And when you get back, our deal is done."

Shards of broken glass gritted under my boot heel as I walked past him. Colón stood and matched his steps to mine as we neared the restaurant's entrance. When I grasped the door knob, he thrust his hand toward me, waist high. "Ask Crystal, ask anybody. Think of me as a bad man, if you want. But my word is good."

I took his hand, squeezing the pudgy fingers until he winced. "Same here, Colón. The promises I make are the ones I keep. I'll get your girls to Tampa safely. When the job is done, we're through."

"Move, Rook!"

Crystal Figueroa's greeting was rough as corrugated iron. But warm too, like I was the dim-witted cook delaying the wagon train in a cowboy movie. Limping, mumble-mouthed, comic, but essential. "What took you so long, *guapo*? You and Martin must have been gossiping like old ladies."

Steamy shadows at the corner darkened the white Prius to molten lilac. In the gloom, a smirk twisted the little killer's face. She hadn't turned her head when I approached, continuing to stare through the windshield at the passing traffic, clogged and slow even after eleven at night.

"Lots of story-telling, Crystal. Lots of promises." Swallowing hurt and the words scratched my throat. If she caught the hoarseness, she didn't say anything.

"Well, whatchu waiting for? Hop in. Let's hit the road." She glanced over the seat and I bent to look at the baby carrier in the rear. A chubby toddler wrapped in pink slumped there, perspiration twinkling on her nose. Black curls were plastered in a neat row under a pink hairband festooned with knit roses. The child's skin shone like polished silver. She was sleeping, her lips pursed into a tight pink bud.

"JoJo's beautiful, ain't she?" The rasp in Crystal's voice was almost maternal. Like sandpaper cooing over an emery board.

Before I could answer, a slim shade murmured beside me: "She's lovely, Crystal. Looks just like you." Brina's whisper startled a yelp from me. Her amber and fresh green scent lifted my heart. I'd never been so happy to see a person in my life.

But I squeezed that soft sentiment out of my voice with the next bark. "The hell, Brina! What're you doing here?"

"You think I'd miss this road trip?" Brina followed me to the driver's side and opened the rear door. "Not a chance."

I clamped my hand over hers. "You can't go with us!"

"Why not? I got my red Bermuda shorts, an extra t-shirt, my Beretta, and three pairs of panties. I'm all set."

"How'd you know what was happening?"

Brina grimaced. My idiocy had sunk below even her ankle-high expectations. "For an old lady, Mei Young has sharp ears. She hid in the kitchen and heard the first sentences of your conversation with Colón. Something about driving to Tampa. Then she called me."

Tough guy voice to counter the thumping heart and clutching throat: "Brina. Listen to me. You can't come." Rude and she'd pay attention. "No argument. No way."

"I've never been to Florida. Now's my chance." Brina's lips, usually so plump and inviting, flattened in determination. "You're not cheating me out of a visit to Magic Mouse World, Mister Detective. No way." An echo to end the discussion.

She threw a canvas duffel behind the driver's seat, then turned to face me again. Pulling an elastic band from her wrist, she raised her arms to gather her springy hair into a top-knot. The simple gesture–biceps flexing, bare throat quivering–defeated me. My tough guy stance buckled under pressure.

Stirring at the noises, the baby burbled, then smacked her lips. Vicious gangsters scared me. Tough landladies too. But the fury of an awakened baby turned my guts to library paste. If JoJo started screaming, these women would nail my eight toes to the sidewalk and mow me down. So, I cooed like a dove on Ambien, hoping to keep the sleeping princess peaceful: "Shoosh, shoosh…" It worked. JoJo slept on.

I had only one argument left. A weak one, but I launched it anyway: "Who'll take care of Herb?"

"The cat will be fine. I already texted Daddy. He's got a key to your place." Shadows couldn't hide the way Brina's soft eyes glimmered under her fluttering lashes.

Crystal leaned across the console to growl through the driver's side window. "She's right, Rook. Your lady's been through a lot. She deserves a vacation."

Brina nuzzled my jaw with a promising kiss. Good things might come from this trek: I'd clear my debt to Colón, extend my protective wing over his innocent child, and save Whip too. With Brina beside me, everything was possible. I slipped under the steering wheel and eased the door shut as Brina did the same behind me. Seat belts fore and aft clicked into place. The baby made a soft *puft-puft* sound, but didn't stir when I lit the ignition.

Crystal the gangster muse cast a prophecy against the deep purple sky as I pulled into traffic. "And, you never know, *guapo*. Your lady's gun might come in handy along the way. Let's ride!"

The tiny assassin was right: you never know. But I'd learned something from Whip: the flipside of bravery is confidence. Molding the plausible into the possible is tough work. But it's an honest job, one worth tackling. This could happen. I'd make sure it did.

I pointed the car toward Tampa and floored the gas pedal.

Thank you for reading *Pauper and Prince in Harlem*, the fourth installment in the Ross Agency mystery series, featuring private detective SJ Rook and his colleagues. If you are interested in reading about the southern road trip launched at the end of this book, check out my short story, "The Killer," in the *Chicago Quarterly Review*, Vol. 31.

I want to express my heartfelt gratitude to readers who combed through an early draft of the manuscript for *Pauper and Prince in Harlem*. They provided insight, sensitive criticism, and crucial ideas that shaped the final text. In our conversations, they were kind, supportive, and brave. I also thank my editor, Sarah Monsma, whose many thoughtful suggestions were immensely helpful. Any remaining faults in this book are mine alone.

Like all characters in this novel, Whip is an invention. But the dangers faced by transgender people, especially teens, are real. Homelessness, poverty, violence, and despair are daily challenges for many trans teens in our neighborhoods. Organizations like the Ali Forney Center of New York City help vulnerable L.G.B.T.Q. kids. Learn more at the Center's website, www.aliforneycenter.org

The previous books in this contemporary noir series are *Lost and Found in Harlem*, *Practice the Jealous Arts*, and *Black and Blue in Harlem*. All are available in eBooks and print on Amazon.com. If you enjoyed reading them, please consider leaving an honest review on Amazon and Goodreads. Other readers will appreciate hearing from you. To learn more about these novels, visit my website, "Neighborhood Noir," at www.deliapitts.com and follow me on Instagram on @deliapitts50.

Daunting new cases test Rook and Brina in the upcoming fifth novel in the series, *Murder My Past*. One memory-plagued widow. Two alluring lost wives. Three jealous academic superstars. The deadly mix means danger and remorse for Rook as he navigates the treacherous depths of his personal history. Can he escape the past's lethal undertow to solve twisted murder cases that threaten the future of those closest to him? *Murder My Past* will be released in 2021. Read on for a sneak peek at the intriguing first chapter of the next Ross Agency mystery, *Murder My Past*.

MURDER MY PAST

A Ross Agency Mystery

DELIA C. PITTS

CHAPTER
ONE

Sabrina Ross flung open the trunk of the pink Pontiac and stared into the car's dusty interior. Bubblegum-colored rubber mats covered the floor. What fiend would do that to an innocent vehicle?

"You remember that movie, the old one with JLo and Clooney?" Brina was a detective, my boss, my boss's daughter, and a whole lot more in my life. When she spoke, I listened.

I stopped fiddling with the cell phone. "Yeah, I never could figure out how two grown adults fit into the trunk of a car."

"Unless they're dead." She holstered her gun in the waistband of her jeans. I poked more digits into the phone. Norment Ross, Brina's dad, wasn't answering. She took off her denim jacket and threw it into the trunk. "Yeah, well unless you've got a better idea, I say we hide in here. We're running out of time." Shouts from the warehouse at the far end of the parking lot grew louder. "I'll get in first. Then you...*Hey*!"

I launched backwards into the trunk, grabbing her wrist as I fell. She landed hard on the rubber mats. I slammed the hood shut two seconds after she snatched her sandals inside. "I *told* you *I'd* get in first! What the *hell* is wrong with you, Rook?"

I jutted my chin into the top of her head. "Shut. Up. Now."

Male voices in multiple languages converged on the car. Spanish, Portuguese from Newark's Ironbound district, some kind of Slavic, and a Vietnamese-accented command voice. Crime in Harlem was an equal opportunity business.

My arms tightened around Brina's back and she pressed her face into my chest. Sunlit amber of forest paths pricked my nose, her fresh scent mingling with sweat and the tang of blood. Her lip was split, matching my eyebrow. We were in a fix.

Angry shouting swelled, the slits of light around the keyhole flickering as the men passed by. Then all fell silent. We waited several moments in the dark, listening to our breaths even out. I reached over her shoulder to push on the trunk door. It was locked. I muttered a curse into the thick rows of braids above her temple.

"Looks like we may be here for a while." Her voice rumbled through my chest, amused rather than pissed off. I was the one who was ticked. When I didn't answer, she chirped. "I thought you were calling Daddy."

"He didn't pick up." Her father was the head of our little neighborhood detective firm, the Ross Agency. He'd sent us to collect against an overdue bill. Sixteen months without one dollar paid was too much even for Norment's over-generous soul. That assignment led to our confrontation with the multi-culti gang in the warehouse. And to our retreat to this goddamned pink car trunk.

"Well, call him again." She let out a huge yawn. "In the meantime, it feels good to rest."

"The phone's somewhere in here. But with you taking up so much space, I can't move enough to find it." Dammit, was she smirking? "You can't catch up on your sleep right now. Roll over." I pushed her shoulder. "Maybe you can feel the phone."

She squirmed, shifting to face the trunk opening, and patted the floor mats. Grainy, sticky, wet, rubbery. But no phone. My knees pressed behind her thighs. I adjusted my shoulder to cover hers. Might as well make the best of the close situation, George Clooney style. She relaxed into me and I rested my hand on her hip. "Sorry, it's tight in here."

"I can't feel the phone." She shoved at the hood. Maybe it would open by magic. Two sharp raps from her fist. Or by brute force. Nothing. We lay for what could have been minutes or only seconds.

My hand grew heavy on her hip, not pressing, but firm and still. "A little privacy, a little quiet." I whispered across her ear, its rim warm under my lips.

"Rook, I love you and all that." She squeaked, a giggle bubbling inside the cheek next to mine. "We work together, help each other, save lives. We're a great team. But I'm not trying for any of *that* mess in the trunk of a damn car!"

"But it's got pink floor mats!" I chuckled. "Brina, relax. You're safe from funky flirtation." My stomach molded against her ass, my fingers increasing the pressure on her hip. Dipping my face to the soft bend between her shoulder and neck, I inhaled. "You smell good. Now, no talking."

She yawned and lowered her head to the grimy mat. I waited for more movement, her stillness spooking me. I was about to speak again, when her jaw slackened. I touched my palm to her cheek. Through open lips breath came moist and familiar on my skin. Sleeping. As if we were in my bed on a Saturday night after pizza and beer. Sleeping. The beautiful bastard. I was trapped in a goddamn car with this gorgeous woman snoring softly in my arms. I couldn't turn, couldn't move. Didn't want to.

———————

The slits around the key hole darkened. Night in August dropped late and sudden, like a heavyweight boxer's knockout blow. But sleep didn't come, so I counted her dear heartbeats. Strong, slow, steady as a river they came, thudding against my chest until I lost track of time. I counted past three hundred, maybe three fifty. She twisted, rolling her head, moans rumbling in mournful waves. "Reggie. No, Reggie."

I tightened my hand around her arm, then stroked her cheek. "Brina, hey. It's alright, you're alright. Wake up, you're safe." She startled, struggling to sit. I clamped my hand on her scalp, my fingers slotted between the rows of braids. "You okay? You can't sit up, you know."

"Yeah, I'm okay." She sniffed and shrugged to ease the stiffness in her back. The key hole was still dark; it felt like we'd been trapped for hours.

I slipped my hand from her hip to rest it against her stomach. The t-shirt was damp with sweat, sticking to the spirals of her belly button. She softened under my touch.

"Who's Reggie?"

"You know who he is."

"Old boyfriend." I answered my own question.

"You know all about my past. Why bother to *ask* me anything?" The shudder reverberating through her body would have emerged as a sob if she hadn't held it in.

I pressed my mouth to her earlobe. "Yeah, I know lots of things *about* you, Brina. About your past. But I want to know you. From you." I pushed on before she could object. "Sure, I know Reggie. He owns a chain of dry cleaners. He's put a big down payment on a brownstone in Jersey City. His wack Afro and his Chivas Regal are straight from the Eighties and he talks too fast. I know these things, but I don't know how you feel."

She laughed and placed her hand over mine, pressing it against her stomach. "Would you stick around if you had me all figured out? I don't think so!"

———————

I outlined her throat with kisses, and she laughed again. The cell buzzed, a rude hum against my ribs. I skated my fingers over the slick face until the line opened, then fumbled the phone to my mouth. "Norment? That you? Where *are* you, man!"

"No. Not Norman. Or whatever you said." A silky female voice drawled through the electronic crackle. *"Is that you, SJ?"*

I knew that purr. Low, leather tough, devious, enticing. "Annie! Where are you?" My ex-wife's voice hadn't changed since high school.

"No need to shout, SJ. I'm right here in New York."

"You're here? Where? How?" Stupid, but still better than croaking like a strangled frog.

"Continental Regent Hotel. For the week. Meet me tomorrow in the bar for drinks." An order, not an invitation.

"Sure, Annie. What time?"

"Eight-thirty too late?"

"No. Fine. I'll be there."

Annie hung up. Silence. No greeting, no explanation. No adiós or good night. Silence. Payback for the last seven years of our mean marriage. And the three dark years since our divorce.

Brina jumped on the case. "Who was that? Didn't sound like a wrong number."

"Ex-wife. Anniesha Perry. She's in town for the week." My heart thumped against Brina's spine.

"She's from Texas, right?"

"No. Florida. Miami." I swallowed the groan rising from my gut. I wasn't having this conversation here. Or anywhere in the known universe. My past could stay past. For at least one more day. "Brina, we gotta get out of here. Now." Was that squawk really my voice?

She turned her head; moonlight filtered past the key hole and the edges of the trunk's hood. Jutting from her braids, a slender metal hook grazed my face.

"Hey! You poked me in the eye with that idiot hairpin!" I sucked breath with the sudden revelation. "Give it to me. Now." With a few twists, I tugged the bobby pin from her braid. I hummed as I demolished it. "Switch places with me."

Brina rolled under me. She snickered as I balanced on knuckles and toes over her. Not going to crush my boss. Unless absolutely necessary. Code of a gentleman, a soldier, *and* a private eye. I worked the hairpin into the key hole and the damn lock surrendered after a few strokes.

I eased from the trunk, unfolding the cramped muscles in my torso and stretching my arms toward the sky. I grabbed Brina's hand and pulled her out. A smirk creased her face in the humid moonlight. She retrieved her jacket, stained with oil and sludge from the floor of the trunk. As she brushed cellophane insect wings from her t-shirt, I punched Norment's number again. Success.

Out of the cloud-pink past, a woman ambled into a ritzy bar. A guy dropped his jaw, his wallet, his pants. Not necessarily in that order. Rollercoaster soared, swooped, crashed. Again.

Anniesha Perry, wife of my youth, was the female. I was the guy. This swanky hotel saloon was the rollercoaster's latest stop. Since high school, I'd balanced on that fine summit where all the time and sex and money and laughter in the world were mine to take. I'd crashed, of course. Many times before I reached forty. Our divorce was three years old, after seven years of married strife. But the carnival ride still circled. Not past enough.

Working as a private investigator in New York toughened me against the soaring and crashing. Right? Grew a turtle's horny shell for skin. And tied a gristle knot where my heart used to beat. Sure. After two years tackling the grit and grief of neighborhood cases, Harlem sophistication dusted my shoulders. Right? Wrong.

The bar Annie picked was the jewel in a mid-town fortress of luxury I'd never enter on my own. The Continental Regent hotel was host to a week-long conference on twenty-first century entrepreneurship. Three thousand people jammed into the glittering pile for the meeting. Tuesday night after her call, I scanned the conference program online. Anniesha Perry was the convention's biggest deal: keynote speaker at the plenary session and a featured participant on several panels. In her photo, Annie wore a sunrise-pink blouse, a thin gold chain nestled in the notch of her throat. The bio under the glossy picture said she owned a Miami cleaning service which reeled in a million dollars a year.

A million. I was lucky to make five hundred dollars in a good week of detecting. Being a private eye was gratifying, but the rewards were non-financial. I liked solving puzzles, fixing problems, restoring order in the neighborhood. I was good at my job: tough on bad guys, sweet to old ladies, stingy with words, quick with fists. The combination played to my strengths. My business was long on danger and boredom, short on money. Since our high school days in San Marcos, Texas, I'd known Annie was out of my league. Now the black ink of her company's ledger offered proof positive.

Annie said eight-thirty. At eight-ten I arrived at the Continental Regent to settle my nerves and case the scene. Wednesday evenings in mid-August were slow; the saloon was stocked with tourists in mint green shorts, damp t-shirts, wrinkled shifts, and white sneakers. Posh regulars had bounced to the Hamptons or Martha's Vineyard. I kept my urban cred by wearing the same black trousers and black button-down shirt I always wore. My poverty could pass for elegance in these circumstances.

I stepped from the bright lobby into the shadows of the Argent Bar. The hostess strutted around a podium, holding a menu at chest height like a shield. Her suit of silver sequins and navy velvet matched the décor of the lounge. Chrome, aluminum, and gray-stained oak floors chilled the room. Blue globe lamps hung from the ceiling like tear drops, shedding sad light. Some of the tear drops gelled into little blue tables scattered around the room. A long slab of blue marble anchored the bar to the right of the entrance. Indigo leather wrapped bar stools, chairs, booths, and benches.

The hostess was tall, with gingerbread hair divided by a severe part. She blinked her china-blue eyes fast, like she regretted my entrance. Regretted my existence, really. I showed my teeth, polished special for her. She steered me to a thumbtack-size table near the kitchen door. I walked past the insult, pointing to the biggest padded booth. The rear of the room had advantages: out of traffic lanes, easy to scan the space, hard to be taken by surprise.

The only other black guy in the place was the piano player. Simple to see why the hostess was uneasy: one black guy was okay; two black guys equaled a gang. If a third black guy arrived, we'd be a race riot. The hostess flinched. Where did I rate on her private scale of brown-people mayhem? Closer to Mahatma Gandhi or Osama bin Laden? Just north of César Chavez, but south of El Chapo? She measured me:

neighborhood tall, not NBA giant. Lean, but solid enough for an alley fight. Paler than a paper bag, darker than a manila folder. I smiled. The hostess sucked her lower lip until it disappeared. She frowned, but led me to the booth I wanted.

As I marched past, the piano player slanted his chin in recognition of our membership in the brotherhood. Straight-faced, I nodded. He strummed the first chords of the French national anthem for my tiny victory. Not gaudy, but loud enough to make the brandy snifter on the piano jiggle. The hostess flinched and retreated to her podium near the door.

A wide doughy girl with string-cheese hair patrolled my zone of the lounge. She grinned approval of my seating choice, like she was lucky to be my waitress. I ordered a club soda, zero booze before Annie arrived. Sloshed was no way to start the meeting. *Why'd Annie pick a goddamn bar for our reunion? Was the saloon a test? A threat? A dare?* This dry wait might kill me. Maybe that was Annie's goal: murder me with sobriety.

Sure, I wanted to see her. But I wanted a drink too. Straight and sober was good. But I also needed to calm my jangling head. The waitress sensed my jam. She prowled the aisle, shooting dewy glances at me, waving her pencil in my direction. As if her plush hips could lure me into ordering the bourbon she promised to pour just for me. I could taste the dose, smoky and soothing against my tongue. But this time, things would be different. I'd be sober for Annie, this time. I shook off the luscious waitress.

Being blitzed had its upside. Easy for Annie to recognize me. Buzzed and familiar. Once a drunk, always a drunk. But I'd show her I'd changed, that the past didn't own me. If she asked for a cocktail, I'd order my usual Beam on the rocks. If she laid off, I would too. Cheese-Hair brought the club soda I requested. She dropped two coasters on the table, white squares of cardboard with a blue circle around "Argent" scrawled in silver letters. On one coaster, a handwritten phone number beckoned. I appreciated the offer, but when she turned her back, I tore the coaster into five strips.

The club soda worked for a while; its clear fizz pious, clean. The lemon's acid cut. But after fifteen minutes and three passes from the waitress, I craved a real drink. Brown liquor to smooth the edges and oil the rusty patches. Wet palms and anxious frowns were a punk's look. But it was the only look I had. Too late to switch.

Then Annie stepped out of my past and into the bar, beautiful as ever. She wore a short pink dress and makeup in the right places. I hated lipstick on her; she'd remembered, so her mouth was naked, the plum color of her flesh melting to rosy pink at the center of her lower lip. I sucked a long gulp from the club soda. All tension erased; all doubt cancelled, our past null and void. As I swallowed, I held the glass at my lips. The coaster stuck to the bottom of the tumbler, a mask shielding my face.

The past had cheated me–of my health, my happiness, my future. Did Annie's arrival promise I'd win this time? Surefire cinch.

The coaster fell.